fairy dust

Gwyneth Rees

Illustrated by Annabel Hudson

MACMILLAN CHILDREN'S BOOKS

First published 2003 by Macmillan Children's Books
a division of Macmillan Publishers Ltd
20 New Wharf Road, London N1 9RR
Basingstoke and Oxford
Associated companies throughout the world
www.panmacmillan.com

ISBN 0 330 41554 9

15 17 19 18 16 14

A CIP catalogue record for this book is available from
the British Library.

Printed and bound in Great Britain by Mackays

fairy dust

Gwyneth Rees is half Welsh and half English and grew up in Scotland. She went to Glasgow University and qualified as a doctor in 1990. She is a child and adolescent psychiatrist and has worked in several places, including Birmingham and London. She now works part-time in order to write and is the author of the amazing *Mermaids* series and, for older readers, the warm and moving *The Mum Hunt*, winner of the Younger Novel category of the Red House Children's Book Award 2004. She lives in London with her two cats.

*To Cameron MacPherson Christie
and the wee man of Caroy Cottage*

Rosie MacLeod ran down the lane to Thistle Cottage while her mother, Maggie, went to collect the key from Miss MacPhee, the old lady who lived next door. Over the hedge she could see across the fields to Loch Shee. It was a beautiful day and the loch was a clear blue colour.

The front door of Thistle Cottage was painted light blue and there was a massive knocker on it in the shape of a pixie's head. Rosie peered in at the window. Something was moving on top of the big oak table in the kitchen. What was it? She pressed her nose against the glass in order to see more closely.

Just then her mother's car rolled in down the driveway. 'Miss MacPhee says to watch out for the fairies!' her mother laughed as she climbed out of the car. 'I'd forgotten how some of the old island people believed in them. You'll fit in very well here, Rosie.'

Rosie had seen fairies once when she was sick in bed with chicken- pox. Her mother had said that her  mind was playing tricks because she had a fever and, no matter how hard she tried, Rosie hadn't been able to convince her mother that the fairies were real.

'Come on, let's go inside,' Mum said, slipping the key into the lock and turning it. 'Miss MacPhee says she had a cleaner in yesterday so it should be spick and span.'

'I thought I saw something moving around in the kitchen just now,' Rosie said.

'Yikes! I hope we haven't got mice,' her mum grimaced. 'If we have, we'll need to borrow Miss MacPhee's cat. She's got an enormous ginger tom called Angus and she says the fairies are always pestering him and pulling his tail. Really, Rosie, I think Miss MacPhee is a little . . . you know . . .' She made a circle with one finger at the side of her head to indicate *crazy*.

Rosie sighed. Just because her mother had never seen a fairy, she didn't believe that *anyone* had.

After they had unloaded the car, her mum went upstairs to put the sheets on their beds while Rosie made sandwiches for supper.

That cleaner didn't do a very good job, she thought. There were crumbs and little blobs of red jam all over the table, which was strange since Miss MacPhee had said that nobody had rented out this cottage since last summer.

In a way, Rosie felt like *they* were just renting out this cottage for the summer too. She had to keep reminding herself that they were here to stay. Rosie couldn't believe that her mum and dad had split up. And now Dad was all alone in London while Rosie and her mother had moved up here to the Isle of Skye in Scotland. It seemed like she would hardly ever *see* Dad from now on. When Rosie had said that to her mum before they'd come here, her mother had said that they never saw him anyway because he spent all his time at work. Rosie hadn't said anything else because her mother had looked as though she was about to start crying. Her mum cried a lot lately.

Rosie's mother was Scottish and Rosie knew that she had only moved down to England in the first place because Rosie's dad, James, worked as a lawyer in London. He worked very hard and he often didn't have time to do things with Rosie and her mum. That was one of the things her parents had argued about a lot.

After tea, Rosie stood her photograph of her father on the little dressing table in her room. Then she went down to the hall to fetch the rest of her things. She had surprised her mother by insisting they bring her old, wooden, dolls' cot with them. She hardly ever played with her dolls any more, but the cot was special because her dad had built it for her when she was very little and her mum had made the covers for it. Rosie didn't care if the yellow paint was flaking off in places and one of the covers was ripped. She still hadn't wanted to leave it behind.

Rosie put the cot down underneath the window and sat down on her bed. She suddenly felt very tired. Maybe she would wait until tomorrow to put everything away.

'I'm sure you'll like it here, darling,' Mum said when Rosie went into her bedroom to say goodnight.

Rosie didn't reply. She was watching her mother hanging up her clothes in the small old-fashioned wardrobe. It made her think about the modern mirror-fronted wardrobe in her parents' bedroom at home and how her dad had always complained about how much space her mother's clothes took up compared to his. 'Dad will have too *much* room for all his stuff now,' she said.

Her mum nodded. 'I expect he'll be pleased about that.'

Rosie didn't say anything, but she didn't think he would.

'What will we do tomorrow?' she asked her mother because, for some reason, the idea of tomorrow scared her a bit now that they were so far away from everything and everyone she was used to.

Her mother gave her shoulders a squeeze. 'We'll go exploring,' she said. 'It'll be fun!'

Rosie went to bed feeling a bit happier and it didn't take her long to fall asleep.

The room was lit by moonlight when Rosie woke up again a few hours later. She was very sleepy and she thought at first that she must be dreaming.

It was a wonderful dream! There, flying above her bed, was a tiny fairy girl. The fairy was keeping a safe distance away from her but was peering at her curiously just the same.

And Rosie suddenly felt wide awake!

She lay very still, holding her breath. She knew how easy it was to frighten fairies away if you let them know you had seen them. This fairy had piercing blue eyes and gold hair caught up in a big bushy ponytail on top of her head. She wore a little silk bodice and a skirt made out of white flower petals. Her wings, fragile as insect wings, fluttered behind her.

Just then, a cross little Scottish voice sounded from the corner of the room. 'Och, it's just plain *mean* of Flora to rent out my cottage!'

Rosie saw that the voice belonged to a little man the same size as the fairy. He also had wings and he hovered beside the top shelf in the little alcove in the wall, where he was packing things into a matchbox. He was dressed in a pleated tartan kilt and matching tartan socks which almost reached his kilt. In between, Rosie could just make out a pair of pink, hairy knees. On his top half, he wore a smart little black velvet jacket, with long sleeves and tiny pearl buttons, over a white shirt and tartan tie. On his head sat a tartan bonnet with a miniature thistle stuck in it, his

red hair poking out from underneath. His eyes were bright green and his face looked like the kind of face Rosie had always imagined on a cheeky elf or pixie.

The matchbox he was packing wasn't closed properly and a tartan sock and a pair of white long johns were poking out of one end.

'Shush! You'll wake her,' the fairy whispered. 'She's got such a nice face – look!'

'I thought you'd come here to help me pack, Snowdrop – not to look at *her*!' the little man grumbled, flying over to take a closer look at Rosie who quickly pretended to be asleep. It wasn't that she was scared of fairies, but she had never seen a fairy man before and this one certainly didn't seem very friendly.

'Look!' Snowdrop said excitedly. 'She's got some wonderful toys. I'd love to come here to play.'

8

'Children may still *look* sweet but they're not as much fun as they were in the old days,' the little man said gloomily. 'All they're interested in now are their computers and their video games. They never want to play with *us* any more.' He flew back to his shelf. 'Now – are you helping me with this or not?'

They flew over Rosie, carrying the matchbox between them, as they headed for the open window.

And by the time Rosie had plucked up the courage to introduce herself, they were gone.

The next morning Rosie woke up with the sun streaming through her window, half sure that she had dreamed the whole thing. She knew that her mother would certainly think that if she told *her* about it.

Rosie looked out of her window at the sparkling blue loch which her mother had told her eventually joined up with the sea. Her mum had also said there were seals and sometimes even dolphins who swam into the loch and loved to show off to any humans who happened to be on the shore. Rosie couldn't wait to go down to the rocky loch-side and explore.

But her mother hadn't slept very well and she wanted to rest for a while longer. 'Why don't you go and have a look round by yourself?' she suggested, sleepily.

10

So Rosie went back into her room and started to look for her shoes, which she'd kicked off the night before. As she knelt down to look under the bed she saw something small and red lying on the carpet.

She picked it up. It was a tiny tartan sock.

She hadn't been dreaming after all!

She nearly ran straight back into her mother's room to tell her everything, but she stopped herself when she imagined what her mum might say. She put the sock in her pocket and went outside. It was a lovely warm day and Rosie skipped up the lane feeling happy. At the top of the driveway she went to unlatch the big farm gate. Then she decided it would be more fun to climb over it. The gate was painted black and as Rosie perched on the top with one leg on either side, she let herself imagine that she was riding a jet-black, wild pony.

'Giddy-up!' she told the gate and she swung one leg over to join the other so that she was riding side-saddle like a proper lady. There was no one here to see her so she could act as silly as she liked!

Then she noticed a large ginger cat sitting on the grassy bank. The cat clearly thought that she was very silly indeed, judging by the way he was looking at her. She jumped off the gate and went over to him.

'Are you Angus?' she asked. The cat gave a slight purr and immediately lifted his chin up so that she could stroke underneath it, which made him purr even more. Rosie saw that attached to his collar was a shiny silver bell. 'I expect that's to stop you catching too many birds, isn't it?' she said.

Angus yawned, as if it didn't bother him in the slightest whether he caught any birds or not. Then he noticed a butterfly fluttering nearby and leaped up to give it an energetic swipe.

'Angus! Where are you?' a crackly voice called out. 'Your breakfast is ready.' And a very old lady with a wrinkly face and grey hair appeared at the top of the lane opposite.

12

'Hello,' Rosie said, jumping up. 'Are you Miss MacPhee?'

The old lady gave a little start as if Rosie were some sort of goblin rather than a perfectly ordinary child. 'Hmm . . .' she said. 'I suppose you're the girl. Your mother didn't tell me she'd be letting you out on your own. I hope you're not upsetting Angus.'

'Well . . . no . . . I was only stroking him,' Rosie stammered.

'Good. Now, Angus, I've your bacon and eggs all ready for you . . . Yes, I know you only like the yolk . . . There's no need to look at me like that.' She started to open the gate, as Angus clearly wasn't going to join her voluntarily.

'Does your cat really like bacon and eggs?' Rosie asked, wide-eyed.

'Well, of course he does! I wouldn't cook it for him if he didn't,' Miss MacPhee said impatiently. The old lady swung the gate open and started heading towards Angus. She was thin and a little bent over but she walked quite smartly.

Rosie remembered what her mother had told her about Miss MacPhee believing in fairies. There was something she badly wanted to know and she couldn't think who else to ask. 'I found this in my bedroom,' she said, pulling the little sock out of her pocket.

Miss MacPhee glanced at it. 'It probably belongs to that pesky wee devil who's been living there all winter making a mess of the place. Every time I go in there I see crumbs and jam and goodness knows what else. He's been having parties in there if you ask me – trying to impress those fairies!'

Rosie swallowed. 'Have *you* seen the fairies, then?'

'Well, of course I have. How could I live here for nearly eighty years and *not* see them?' Miss MacPhee took the sock from Rosie. 'Oh, yes. This belongs to one of the wee men, all right – you can tell which one if you look at the tartan.' She held it up and peered at it more closely. 'Och, it's no good – I can't see properly without my glasses.'

'Could we go into the house and *get* your glasses?' Rosie asked, shyly. She was longing to know which wee man the sock belonged to.

'Well . . .' Miss MacPhee looked suspicious. 'I don't usually let children into my house, you know . . . One never knows what they might get up to.'

Rosie sighed. Miss MacPhee was obviously far more used to fairies than she was to children. Rosie put the sock back in her pocket. 'It's just that I've never seen a wee man before,' she said. 'Are they a sort of fairy?'

Miss MacPhee chuckled. 'Aye, they're that all right – though they don't like to be *called* fairies. *That* makes them very cross! Wee men only live in Scotland – well, they'd look quite out of place anywhere else – and they like to think they're cleverer than the fairies. Now that isn't true but the fairies let them pretend it is, just to keep them happy. And because the fairies make the wee men so happy, they do all sorts of things to help the fairies in return.'

'What sort of things?' Rosie asked, fascinated. But Miss MacPhee had scooped up Angus and was heading back down the lane with him. Rosie desperately wanted to ask one more thing. 'Miss MacPhee?' she called out. But apparently Miss MacPhee was a bit deaf when she had her back turned because she didn't reply.

Rosie followed her and caught up with her at the front door of her cottage. The door was open and a smell of bacon was coming from the house. Angus immediately struggled out of Miss MacPhee's arms and disappeared inside.

'Miss MacPhee, do you know how I could get the fairies to come back?' Rosie asked, breathlessly. 'There was one called Snowdrop.'

'Snowdrop?' Miss MacPhee laughed. 'Well, if you want to tempt that wee madam, the best thing to use is her sweet tooth. She can't resist chocolate.'

'*Chocolate?*' Rosie had never thought about fairies liking chocolate before. 'But how will I let Snowdrop know I've got some for her?'

'You've got a window ledge, haven't you?' Miss MacPhee answered impatiently. 'Well, use it! Fairies are always checking to see what folk have left for them on their window ledges.' And she went inside her house and shut the door.

Slowly, Rosie walked up the lane and back to Thistle Cottage where her mother was now in the kitchen making breakfast. She waved to Rosie through the window and Rosie waved back.

Chocolate, she thought. Well, that should be easy enough. Her auntie in London had given her a box of chocolates before she left. She would choose one of the big strawberry creams wrapped in silver foil and leave it with the little sock on her window ledge tonight.

Then, all she had to do was stay awake and wait for the fairies to come back!

That evening, Rosie waited until her mother had gone to the door to shake the crumbs off the tablecloth before slipping her hand into the chocolate box which she had been allowed to open after supper. Rosie had already had four chocolates herself, which her mum said was enough for one night or she'd be sick, but this last chocolate wasn't for her. It was for Snowdrop.

Upstairs in her bedroom, she opened her window and carefully placed the chocolate on the outside ledge with the little tartan sock tucked firmly under it. She left the window open and the curtains pulled back so she had a clear view of the night sky outside. The moon was shining brightly and Rosie reckoned it was just the sort of evening when she would want to go out and about exploring if *she* was a fairy.

She heard her mother climb up the stairs and go into her bedroom across the landing. They had spent a lovely day together, walking over the fields down to the loch-side where they'd gone paddling. Rosie's mum had showed her how to skim stones across the loch, and then she'd got very excited as she spotted a grey shiny head, which turned out to be a seal, bobbing about in the water. Rosie hadn't seen her mum this happy in a long time and seeing her so excited made Rosie feel excited too. Maybe it would be fun here after all.

But Rosie was tired from all the walking they'd done today. Her eyelids were feeling very heavy and soon it was all she could do to keep one eye open to watch the window ledge. She could make out the silver foil glittering in the moonlight and just hoped Snowdrop would spot it too. She started to think about the seal they had seen today. It had followed them in the water as they walked along the loch-side. Her mother had said that seals often did that because they were quite nosy and liked the sound of human voices.

Rosie had looked out across the water at the seal whose smooth head could still be seen above the blue-grey water. 'I wish he'd come closer. I'd like to stroke him!'

'We might get closer if we went out in a boat,' her mum said. 'Miss MacPhee has a little rowing boat which she rents out to people who stay in the cottage. I could ask her about taking it out. Would you like that?'

'Oh, yes!' Rosie had nodded excitedly.

Now, as she lay in bed with her eyes closed, she was imagining bobbing up and down in the water in a little boat with the seal bobbing up and down alongside her. And suddenly the seal was gone and her father was there swimming along beside the boat and Rosie was reaching out to grab his hand to pull him inside. In her dream, Rosie smiled as she sat in the boat with her mum and dad, eating chocolates.

*

The next morning Snowdrop's chocolate was gone and so was the little tartan sock. Rosie was furious with herself for falling asleep and missing the fairies. She flung on her clothes and ran downstairs to check outside the cottage, just to make sure that the chocolate and the little sock hadn't somehow fallen off the ledge during the night. She was searching in the flower bed in front of the house when her mother called out to her. Her mother was sitting out in the garden painting and, judging from how much work she'd already done, she must have got up very early. Her mother had sold lots of paintings when they'd lived in London. There was a gallery there which often displayed them and Rosie knew that her mother had promised to send them some of the paintings she did here. Her mum also thought she might be able to sell some paintings to the tourists who came to Skye to visit and she was even talking about setting up her own little art gallery here on the island.

'Rosie, it's such a lovely day!' her mother said, as Rosie stood behind her, admiring her painting of the loch. 'Why don't you go and ask Miss MacPhee if we can take her boat out? Ask her how much it is and tell her I'll pay her later.'

'Oh, Mum! Can't *you* ask her?' Rosie didn't like the thought of having to go and face Miss MacPhee again.

'I want to finish this. It would help me if you did it. Besides, it's good for you to speak to people. I don't want you becoming too shy.'

Well, why did you bring me up here, where there *aren't* any people, then? Rosie felt like asking. But just then she spotted something shiny on the ground. She bent down to see what it was and let out an excited gasp. It was the scrunched-up silver foil paper from Snowdrop's chocolate!

Miss MacPhee was sitting on the wooden bench outside her cottage, shelling peas. Rosie had never seen anyone shelling peas before. Everyone *she* knew bought their peas from the frozen food section in the supermarket. She couldn't help staring as Flora popped open the big green pods and ran her finger along to push the peas out into the bowl she was balancing on her lap.

'Hello,' Flora greeted her, waving one of

the long green pods at her. 'Want something, do you?'

Rosie quickly gave the old lady the message from her mother about the boat.

Flora nodded. 'Aye, she can take it out if she wants to, so long as you both wear lifejackets. Can she row all right?'

'Yes – and so can I,' Rosie replied proudly. In the summer, she and her mother had often taken out one of the rowing boats in the park near their house in London.

Rosie was turning to leave when Flora called her back.

'Find that Snowdrop, did you?'

Rosie looked back, feeling her cheeks going red. 'I left the chocolate for her like you said but I fell asleep. I think she must have come in the night, though, because the chocolate and the sock were both gone. I found this.' She took the foil wrapper out of her pocket and showed it to Flora.

'That little greedy guts! Had to eat it there and then, all by herself, instead of taking it back to share with the others. She'll have a terrible belly ache this morning and it'll serve her right!'

Rosie's mouth dropped open. 'Do fairies

get belly ache, then?' she asked, hardly believing it.

'Of course they do! They get colds too. There's nothing like a fairy sneeze to give a person a fright. It's the strangest thing you've ever heard. I had a wee man with a cold in my house last winter and I'm telling you – never again! Poor Angus was terrified. And the tissues that went missing.'

'Did he get better?' Rosie asked.

'Och, yes. After I'd been up on that moor collecting sphagnum moss and spending all day boiling it up into a hot toddy for him. Now . . . there's a thought . . .' Miss MacPhee picked up another pea pod. 'I've an idea how you can get to see the fairies. They collect the moss up on the moor because of its special healing properties. They use it for all sorts of things. They go up there very early in the morning just as it starts to get light, so that's when you're most likely to spot one. If you can wake up that early yourself, that is. I know what you city people are like!'

'Of course I can wake up,' Rosie exclaimed. 'Anyway – I'm not a city person any more.' She flushed. 'Mum says to ask you how much it is to hire out your boat.'

Miss MacPhee chuckled. 'Well, if you're not a city person then I can't charge you anything. I only charge the holidaymakers for my boat.' She winked at Rosie. 'You tell your mother she can borrow it whenever she wants, for as long as she's my neighbour.'

Rosie was about to thank her when she spotted Angus sauntering down the path carrying something in his mouth. He was looking very pleased with himself.

'What have you got there?' Flora asked

him. 'Come and show me, then!' Flora stood up slowly and shuffled nearer to him. Then she bent down and made some encouraging noises as if she thought he was the cleverest cat in the whole world and wanted to admire whatever it was he had caught.

As soon as Angus came close enough, she reached out and grabbed him. 'Rosie, see what he's got in his mouth, will you? Be careful now! Watch he doesn't bite you!'

Rosie didn't mind cats usually but she had to admit to being a bit afraid of Angus. But she could see the little bird trapped between his jaws and she really wanted to rescue it. So while Flora held his head still, she carefully prised open his mouth. Angus hissed angrily in protest as the little bird fell to the ground and stayed there, looking stunned.

'Is it hurt?' Rosie asked anxiously.

'I don't think so – just paralysed with fright.' Flora was still clutching Angus. 'Take it away somewhere where Angus won't find it. I expect it'll fly off again when it gets its strength back.'

So Rosie walked carefully back to Thistle Cottage with the little bird balanced on the palm of her hand. Her mother was still in the garden, painting. She stopped as Rosie came towards her. 'Why not put it on your window ledge? It'll be safe there and you can see when it flies away,' she suggested, after she had given the frightened bird a gentle stroke.

So that's what Rosie decided to do. Only, when she got upstairs and opened her window to place the little bird outside, she found something else on her window ledge. It was a bracelet made of flowers, just the right size to fit her wrist. She placed the bird down beside the ring of flowers and, almost immediately, the bird's head gave a little twitch and it looked more alert.

She picked up the bracelet. It was made of tiny flowers of different colours – purple and pink and blue and yellow – woven together in the same way daisies can be strung together to make a daisy chain. Only there was something about it that was different. It was sparkling in the sunshine as if someone had sprinkled it with some type of gold glitter. Rosie slipped the bracelet on to her wrist and ran downstairs.

She could hardly hold in her excitement. She was almost sure the fairies had made the bracelet for her but there was one person who would know for sure.

'I'm going back to see Miss MacPhee for a minute,' she called out to her mother.

'Look!' her mum said, pointing upwards.

And Rosie looked up and smiled as she spotted the bird Angus had caught fly off her window ledge and soar away towards the nearest tree tops.

4

Rosie looked down at her wrist as, the following morning, she hurried up towards the gate that led on to the moor. When she had shown Flora the flower bracelet, the old lady had said that she was almost certain it was a fairy bracelet and that the gold sparkly bits were the fairy dust. 'A *fairy* flower bracelet doesn't wilt until all the fairy dust wears off,' Flora explained. 'So if that's a fairy bracelet, the flowers will stay fresh for a good few weeks.'

Today, the flowers in Rosie's bracelet still looked as if they had only just been picked.

Rosie reached the gate and jumped up on to the first rung. She was getting good at climbing over gates since they'd arrived here. She had set her alarm to make sure she woke up before sunrise this morning. It had been quite dark outside but she knew that if she wanted to see the fairies, she had to be on the moor just as the sun was coming up. It was getting lighter by the minute as she tramped over the bumpy tufts of grass and moss. Flora had said that the fairies lived in the forest, so to head for the mossy ground nearest the trees if she wanted to be sure of spotting one.

It took Rosie longer than she'd thought to reach the edge of the forest. The sun had risen behind the trees by then and there were no fairies in sight. She was beginning to think they must have finished collecting their moss and gone home when she saw a speck of blue moving around in the grass. What was it? A butterfly maybe? Rosie crept closer and saw that the blue colour belonged to something much bigger than a butterfly. It was a huge blue petal and it was making up part of a fairy dress! Rosie held her breath. The fairy wearing the dress was bending over, searching for something in the grass. She had shiny black hair which swung prettily at her shoulders and her delicate wings were half folded behind her, fluttering slightly in the breeze.

Rosie was so excited she couldn't speak.

The little blue fairy suddenly turned

round, let out a frightened gasp when she saw Rosie, dropped the basket of moss she was holding and flew off at top speed into the woods.

'Come back! I'm not going to hurt you!' Rosie called after her in a shaky voice. But the fairy had gone.

Rosie sat down on the ground and carefully picked up the fairy basket. It was made of bark and had a pretty handle woven out of ivy. The basket was full to the brim with fresh moss. The little fairy must have nearly finished collecting it. Perhaps she would come back for it if Rosie waited long enough. Rosie carried the basket of moss over to the edge of the forest and looked for a good place to leave it. There was a tree trunk with a ring of flowers growing round the bottom. The flowers were quite similar to the ones in her bracelet. Rosie left the basket on top of the tree trunk and sat down on the grass a short distance away. Maybe the little blue fairy would come back for the basket and Rosie could tell her that she only wanted to be her friend.

But Rosie waited and waited and the fairy didn't reappear. It was getting late and she knew her mother would be getting up soon. She had to go back to the cottage.

Rosie paused as she was climbing over the rusty old farm gate back out on to the road. She sat on top of the gate, looking around at the green and brown countryside. Her mother had told her that soon the purple heather would be out and it would look even more beautiful. Her mother was always going on about how wonderful it was here and how there were no pollution smells like there were in London. But Rosie didn't remember smelling fumes all the time in London. The smell she remembered best was the smell of the grass just after it had been cut in the park in the summer. For a moment or two she felt sad, remembering the park and the friends she had played with there. They would be playing without her now.

Suddenly she noticed something moving in the long grass on the other side of the road. She saw Angus darting forward and thought he must be trying to catch a butterfly again, but then she heard a loud squeal and a frightened voice shouting, 'Help!'

Rosie leaped down off the gate and ran over. She gasped. Angus had a fairy in his

mouth. Rosie couldn't
see her wings but she
could see her mass of
golden hair and her lit-
tle pink arms and legs,
which were struggling
furiously.

Angus growled, clamp-
ing his jaws shut even tighter as the little
fairy grabbed hold of his whiskers and tugged
at them. Rosie knew she had to do something
fast, but she couldn't think what. Then she
remembered how Miss MacPhee had rescued
the little bird the day before.

Very slowly she crept closer to the cat,
making cooing noises and telling him how
clever he was. Angus looked at her suspi-
ciously but Rosie kept on complimenting him
in a soothing voice. Angus, who found it difficult to resist being praised, started to purr.

'It must be *so* hard to catch a fairy,' Rosie
continued, close enough now to crouch down
in front of Angus who looked as though he
was very proud of himself indeed. '*Please* can I
see?'

Angus opened his mouth to miaow a reply
and the fairy half flew, half tumbled out.

'Go away, Angus!' Rosie shouted, scooping up the fairy and giving the indignant cat a shove with the toe of her wellington boot.

She looked down at the little person in her hand, recognizing her immediately. 'Snowdrop!' she exclaimed.

'Aye, that's my name!' Snowdrop was starting to recover. She sat herself upright in Rosie's hand and dusted off her white petal skirt.

Angus gave them both a disdainful glance and walked haughtily away, seeming more interested suddenly in the smell of fried bacon wafting up from Miss MacPhee's open front door.

'I hope all that fatty food gives you indigestion, you horrible cat!' Snowdrop shouted after him. Then she turned and looked up at Rosie's face. 'You're the little girl from the other night, aren't you? The one who left me the chocolate? You must be because you're wearing my bracelet.' She suddenly smiled. She had pink cheeks and a little pointed chin and her blue eyes were sparkling. 'Thank you for rescuing me!'

'That's . . . OK,' Rosie stammered, suddenly feeling shy.

'What's the matter? You look like you've never seen a fairy before!' Snowdrop grinned.

'It's not that . . .' Rosie said quickly. 'It's just . . . I can't really believe . . . I'm actually *holding* one in my hand.'

Snowdrop laughed. 'I bet you can't even *feel* me sitting on your hand, can you?'

'Well, you do feel ever so light!'

'That's because fairies don't weigh anything,' Snowdrop said. She stretched her wings ready to fly off Rosie's hand, then shrieked in dismay.

'What's wrong?' Rosie asked. Then she saw that there was a big rip in one of Snowdrop's wings where Angus's claw had caught it. 'Oh, no. Can you fix it?' she asked anxiously.

Snowdrop explained that to mend her wing she first needed to make a special poultice. She had to collect some sphagnum moss from the moor to mix with some fairy dust, and if she put that on her broken wing it would mend in a day or two. 'But I'll never be able to fly as far as the moor to collect the moss with my wing like this.'

'Don't worry. I'll collect it for you,' Rosie offered.

Snowdrop looked at her gratefully.

'There's a special kind we have to find. If you carry me up there, I'll show you. I'll need somewhere to rest afterwards, though, while the poultice does its work.' She paused. 'I don't suppose I could sleep in that lovely fairy bed in your room until I'm better, could I?'

'*Fairy* bed?' Rosie couldn't think what she was talking about. Then she realized. 'Oh, you mean my dolls' cot?' she said excitedly. 'Of course you can sleep in it! You can stay as long as you like. Though you'll have to watch my mum doesn't see you. She doesn't believe in fairies so she'd get a terrible fright.'

'Oh, she won't be able to see me,' Snowdrop said dismissively. 'Some people are just *never* in the right mind for seeing fairies.'

'How do you mean?' Rosie was puzzled.

'Well, to see a fairy, you have to be in the right place at the right time in the right *mind*,' Snowdrop explained. 'And lots of humans just never are.'

Rosie still didn't really understand. Right now, though, she was more interested in getting Snowdrop up to the moor and back before her mother woke up and wondered where she was. 'Let's go and get the moss straight away. Then we can go back to the cottage and have some breakfast,' she said.

'Good,' Snowdrop beamed. 'I'm starving! I don't suppose you've got any more of those nice chocolates, have you?'

'I might have,' Rosie laughed, and she headed back towards the moor with her new friend balanced on her shoulder.

5

Rosie stayed inside with Snowdrop for the whole of the next day. The day after that she still hadn't left the house and her mother was starting to get worried.

'You're spending a lot of time in your room, Rosie,' her mother said, taking a break from her painting to put her head round the door. 'What are you doing?'

'Just playing,' Rosie said. She was sitting on the floor beside the dolls' cot, where Snowdrop was sitting eating a slice of cake. Rosie had baked some fairy cakes that morning while her mum was busy painting and she had brought one upstairs for Snowdrop to try.

'With what?' her mum asked, staring at the dolls' cot which, to her, seemed empty.

'Can't you see?' Rosie really wanted her mother to see the fairies too.

Her mother sighed. 'All I can see is you sitting on your own in the house when it's a beautiful day outside. I think you need to get some fresh air. After I've done a bit more painting, we'll go into Portree to do some shopping.'

'I don't want to,' Rosie said. 'I want to stay inside!'

'Rosie—' her mother began, like she was about to deliver a lecture. Then she obviously thought better of it. 'I won't be long, I promise,' she said. 'Then we'll go into Portree.'

'She *will* be long,' Rosie said, stroppily, to Snowdrop after her mother had gone. 'She'll be *ages*. She'll probably be so busy painting, she'll forget all about going to Portree. All she does now is paint.'

'Did she paint all the time before?' Snowdrop asked.

Rosie nodded. 'Mum said it was the only thing that made her feel better when we lived with Dad. They were always arguing. That's why they had to separate.'

'And do they *still* argue?' Snowdrop asked.

Rosie nodded. 'They can't even speak to each other on the phone any more without one of them getting cross.'

Snowdrop looked thoughtful. 'I could fix that, if you want.'

'Fix it?' Rosie stared at her. 'How?'

'I could use a little fairy dust on your mum to put her in a better mood with your father. Then she won't get so angry with him on the phone.'

'Could you really do that?'

'Of course.' Snowdrop twisted round and started to shake off the poultice from her damaged wing. 'This must be mended by now.' She stretched both her wings to test them out, then flew straight up in the air above the cot and hovered there until she was sure her torn wing was properly healed. 'Perfect!' she grinned, starting to fly towards the door.

'Where are you going?' Rosie asked.

'To sprinkle some fairy dust on one of those cakes you made this morning. Then you can take it out to your mother and, when she eats it, she'll start feeling all romantic again towards your dad and she'll totally forget all the things that annoy her about him!'

'But—' Rosie was about to say that she wasn't so sure they ought to make Mum have *romantic* thoughts about Dad, but Snowdrop was already halfway to the kitchen. By the time Rosie caught up with her, Snowdrop was hovering above a cake with yellow icing and an orange jelly tot on top, rubbing the tips of her fingers together and releasing a scattering of golden dust over the icing.

'Wow!' Rosie gasped, as she gazed in awe at the cake which had now started to sparkle. 'But Mum's going to notice that it looks weird!'

'No she won't,' Snowdrop reassured her. 'People who can't see fairies can't see fairy dust either, so don't worry. Just take it out to her. Go on!'

'It won't hurt her, will it?' Rosie asked nervously.

'Of course not! It will just make her think lovely happy thoughts about your dad.'

So Rosie carried the fairy cake carefully outside to where her mother was sitting at her easel, painting a picture of the cottage. 'I've brought one of my cakes for you to try,' she said.

'Oh, thank you, darling. It looks yummy!' Her mother smiled as she took the cake from

Rosie. She put down her paintbrush and peeled the paper cup from round the edges before biting into the sponge and icing. 'Delicious!' she declared, picking up her paintbrush again and continuing to munch as she worked.

Rosie watched her for a few moments, then left her to it.

When her mother came into the house ten minutes later, she looked flushed. She went straight to the kitchen sink and filled herself a glass of water.

'Are you all right, Mum?' Rosie asked.

'I feel as if . . .' her mother faltered, looking confused. 'I feel as if . . .' She raised the glass of water to her mouth with a shaky hand and took a large gulp.

'She feels as if she's fallen in love with your father all over again,' Snowdrop whispered.

'I'm just going to make a quick phone call,' her mother said. 'Then we can go into Portree, OK?'

Rosie nodded. She was so nervous she was starting to feel sick. Was her mother about to ring her father? What would happen if her parents spoke to each other? Would Mum *tell* Dad she felt as though she was in love with him all over again?

The telephone was on the little table in the hallway. It was one of those old-fashioned phones where you put your finger in the holes and pull the dial round once for each number. Her mother went out into the hall and closed the door behind her.

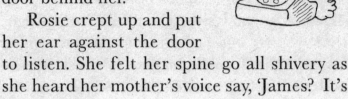

Rosie crept up and put her ear against the door to listen. She felt her spine go all shivery as she heard her mother's voice say, 'James? It's me – Maggie.'

Rosie was so excited and nervous at the same time that she could hardly breathe as she waited to hear what was said next.

'Listen, James, I'm phoning because . . .' Her mum suddenly sneezed. 'Because . . . well . . . because I suddenly really wanted to talk to you.' Her mother sneezed again, louder this time. 'What? Oh . . . but surely . . .' She sneezed again, three times in a row.

'It must be a side effect from the fairy dust,' Snowdrop whispered to Rosie. 'Some humans are a bit allergic to it.'

There was a long silence, broken only by her mother sneezing again, then her voice said, in a stilted sort of tone, 'Well, if they're important clients then, no, I suppose you can't really be late for your appointment with them, but—' She sneezed again. There was another pause while her mother listened. Then she spoke again, clearly angry now. 'Well, I thought that since it was Saturday . . . *Aatchoo!* . . . you *wouldn't* be working, but . . . *Aatchoo!* . . . how silly of me! *Aatchoo!* I forgot that you're *always* working. What? No, I haven't got a cold! *Aatchoo!* It must be the pollen. We have pollen here you know, not filthy petrol fumes . . . . *AATCHOO!'* And she slammed down the phone.

Rosie stared at Snowdrop in horror as she heard her mother running up the stairs. 'Oh, no. We've made everything worse. Mum's really upset now.'

'Oh, dear.' Snowdrop fluttered about anxiously, trying to think of something that would make up for what had happened. 'Rosie, listen! The day after tomorrow there's going to be a special fairy party on the island out on the loch. What if I ask if you can come?'

Rosie stared at her, temporarily forgetting about her mother. 'Come and meet all the other fairies, you mean?'

Snowdrop nodded. 'Queen Mae doesn't usually like us to invite humans to our parties, but when I tell her how you've helped me, I'm sure she'll say yes.'

'Oh, Snowdrop, do you really think she will?' Rosie gasped.

Snowdrop grinned. 'I'll come back and leave her answer on your window ledge tonight. I'll leave a sprig of heather if the answer is yes, and a dandelion if the answer is no.'

As Snowdrop flew away, Rosie crossed her fingers and wished as hard as she could for the answer to be yes.

A fairy party! She could hardly believe it. But before she could get much more excited about it, she remembered how upset her mother had sounded. First she had to go upstairs and see what she could do to make her feel better. And for the umpteenth time, Rosie wished her mother could see the fairies too.

Rosie rushed to her window ledge the next morning and let out an excited shout. A sprig of purple heather was sitting there. Queen Mae had said yes!

The fairy party was going to be held the following night on the island out in the loch. Rosie could hardly wait and she had lots of questions to ask Snowdrop, like how would she get to the island and would Snowdrop come and tell her when it was time to go?

For the whole of the next day, Rosie kept a sharp lookout for her new friend but she didn't appear. Rosie had chosen her favourite purple dress to wear to the party and that night she lay awake waiting for her mother to go to bed, then changed into her party dress and waited. What if Snowdrop had forgotten about her? Or what if she'd changed her mind about taking her to the party?

By midnight Rosie had fallen asleep on top of the bed, still fully dressed, but she woke straight away when she felt something spiky poking at her nose.

'Wake up, Sleepy! It's time to go.' It was Snowdrop, poking at her with the jagged edge of a fairy wand.

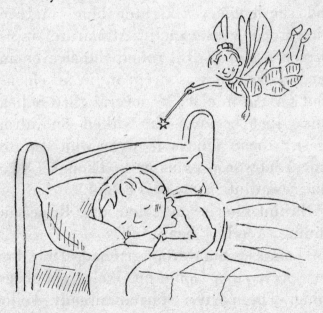

'Wow!' Rosie gasped, staring at the wand which was star-shaped at the end and covered in glittery stuff. 'Is that a *magic* wand?'

Snowdrop glanced down at it. 'Oh, no, this is just to look trendy at the party. It's the fashion for fairies to have wands – though they're a bit of a nuisance to carry around.'

Snowdrop had flown back to the window ledge and Rosie could see her clearly in the moonlight. She wasn't wearing her usual white petal frock. Her skirt was made of several layers of different shades of blue petals and the bodice, a lighter blue, matched Snowdrop's eyes exactly. Miniature daisies formed a sort of frill round the sleeves and her golden hair was swept up in an elegant knot pinned in place by several glittery hairpins. 'Just because I'm called Snowdrop, doesn't mean I have to wear white *all* the time,' Snowdrop explained. 'Though Queen Mae says white *is* my best colour.'

'I think blue is your colour too,' Rosie said, smiling. 'You look beautiful!'

'Thanks,' Snowdrop grinned. 'You look very pretty too. Come on. We've got to get going. The party's started already. Follow me.' She led the way down the stairs and waited for Rosie to open the front door. Then she flew ahead of her down towards the loch.

The moon was so bright that they didn't

need any other light to guide them as they headed down to the loch-side. Rosie could just make out the tiny island in the middle of the water. Her mother had rowed out to the island on the day they had borrowed Flora's boat and there had been nothing there but the ruined remains of a small castle.

'The island just looks the same,' Rosie said, trying not to sound disappointed. Somehow she had expected the island to look different for the fairy party.

'From here it does,' Snowdrop agreed. 'It won't do for much longer, though. Step into the boat.'

Rosie saw that Flora's boat was sitting at the water's edge a short distance away.

She stepped inside, looking around for the oars and wondering how the boat was going to get off the beach – when her mum had taken her out, she had worn her wellingtons and pushed the boat out with Rosie in it.

'Sit down,' Snowdrop ordered, flying behind the boat and pushing it out into the loch with apparently no effort at all. She came and joined Rosie, staring ahead at the island, which still looked deserted and uninviting.

49

There seemed to be no need to row. The boat was moving forward on its own. Behind them Rosie could see a trail of golden sparks in the water that looked like fairy dust.

Suddenly the air was filled with a loud oinking noise and their boat was completely surrounded by seals.

Snowdrop seemed to be able to talk to them. 'Yes . . . I know . . . What? Oh . . . this is my new friend, Rosie. Look after her, will you, while I fly on ahead to tell the others we're coming.'

'Snowdrop, don't—' Rosie started to say, but before she could feel afraid at being left in the boat in the middle of the loch all by herself, she saw some more movement in the water ahead of her. Some dolphins were heading towards her and soon they were right by the boat, jumping out of the water and diving back in again with a splash, then swimming under the boat and resurfacing on the other side. Rosie was so excited at being so close to the dolphins that she nearly didn't spot Snowdrop coming back to hover just in front of her.

'I forgot to tell you,' the fairy said, sounding out of breath. 'To make the island come to life you have to look into the water. There's a magic reflection that will take you there.'

'What reflection?' Rosie called out, but Snowdrop had already flown off again.

The island, which was much closer now, still looked dark and scary to Rosie. What did Snowdrop mean about a magic reflection? Rosie looked into the water and couldn't see anything. Then, just as she was giving up hope, she spotted some twinkling lights. She stared at them. The longer she looked, the more lights seemed to be appearing and then, suddenly, she saw that the lights formed the outline of an upside-down sparkling castle in the water.

'It's upside-down because it's a reflection,' Rosie thought. 'But how can it be a reflection when there isn't anything to reflect?'

She looked up at the island again, just to make sure, and this time she was so shocked that she let out a little cry.

A beautiful castle stood in the middle of the island, looking like something out of a fairy-tale book. It had smooth silvery walls and two round turrets with pointed roofs and tiny windows in the sides. Fairy lights were strung round each turret and there were pink and gold lamps in every window. In front of the castle was a huge courtyard where fairies and wee men were dancing together, inside a ring of lanterns, to lively Scottish fiddle music.

Snowdrop was waiting for her at the end of a narrow wooden jetty. 'Surprised?' she called out, as the friendly seals gave the boat a gentle nudge to line it up with the wooden platform then swam away to join the dolphins who had stayed further out in the loch.

'Is it . . . *real* . . . ?' Rosie stammered, staring

at the jetty and the castle behind it with a feeling that everything might just disappear again at any second.

'Of course it's real,' Snowdrop said. 'Otherwise you wouldn't be able to see it, would you – or stand on it!' She laughed as Rosie stepped nervously on to the creaky platform. 'And whatever you do, *don't* ask if you're dreaming? It's *so* boring when humans ask that.'

Rosie promised that she wouldn't ask that as she followed Snowdrop along the jetty towards the party. But she made sure she pinched herself quickly when Snowdrop wasn't looking, just to make sure.

Rosie hadn't expected the thing that happened next. As soon as Snowdrop led her to the edge of the courtyard where all the fairies were dancing, the music stopped and everyone turned to stare at her.

Rosie felt her face going bright red.

'They're just curious, that's all,' Snowdrop reassured her. 'Come on. I'll take you to meet Queen Mae.'

Rosie felt like a big clumsy giant as she stepped into the courtyard after Snowdrop.

53

Some of the fairies were smiling at her and most of them were whispering to each other as she passed by. One of the wee men lifted his bonnet and gave her a wink.

Snowdrop led the way through the crowd of fairies. Rosie gasped at their beautiful flowery dresses, and at the wee men in their smart tartan outfits. At the back of the court-yard was a very beautiful fairy, sitting on a tree trunk throne that was scattered with gold rose petals. She was wearing a cream silk petticoat with an outer skirt of deep-pink

petals and her bodice was made of woven lavender. Her large wings were spread open behind her, glittering in the moonlight. On top of her wavy, golden hair she wore a purple floral crown. She had the kindest blue eyes and the loveliest smile as she turned to Rosie and said, 'Welcome to our party. And thank you for rescuing Snowdrop and helping her until her wing got better.'

'That's all right,' Rosie said shyly. 'I'm very pleased to meet you, Queen Mae.'

Queen Mae gave her an even more beautiful smile. 'And I, you. Now off you go and enjoy the party. Snowdrop will look after you.'

And Snowdrop did look after her. She sat her on a nice smooth tree trunk up against the courtyard wall where she could watch the fairy party in comfort. Snowdrop brought her a thimble-cup of bubbly-dew to drink, which tasted sweet and made Rosie's tummy feel lovely and warm inside. There was party food to eat too. Snowdrop brought her a plate the same size as the ones in her dolls' tea set at home, and on it were tiny mushrooms stuffed with a delicious herb, pine nut biscuits, miniature fairy cakes with tartan icing and wild berries dipped in honey. Rosie felt very excited as she watched the wee men playing their fiddles and the fairies dancing in groups. Most of the fairies were no longer carrying their wands and Rosie noticed a little heap of them on the floor. Some of the fairies were dancing round it.

Snowdrop was still holding her wand, which she was waving in time to the fiddle music, as she sat beside Rosie, keeping her company.

Just then a wee man came up and gave a little bow to both of them. He wore a bright red bonnet with a tassel on top and he introduced himself as Hughie, of the clan MacDonald. He wanted to know if Snowdrop would like him to carry her wand for her. Snowdrop winked at Rosie as she and Hughie set off to have a wee stroll about the grounds together.

They hadn't been gone long when Rosie was tapped roughly on the shoulder from behind. She turned to see the wee man she had seen in Thistle Cottage on the night she'd arrived. He was flying about inspecting each part of her rudely, as if she was some sort of giant statue, rather than a person.

'So you're the girl who's been staying in my cottage?' he finally said, flapping his wings so close to her face that it made her blink. 'I'm Cammie MacPherson, in case you're interested.'

'I'm Rosie Macleod,' Rosie said, wishing Snowdrop would hurry up and come back. 'And anyway, I thought it was Miss MacPhee's cottage.'

'Old Flora knows very well that I staked my claim on that cottage long ago,' Cammie retorted crossly. 'And she knows I don't like sharing it with any of her tourist folk.'

'I'm not a tourist,' Rosie defended herself. 'And neither is my mum. We live here now.'

Cammie gazed at her in dismay. '*Live* here? You mean you're not going away again at the end of the summer?'

Rosie shook her head. 'Mum says we're going to rent Thistle Cottage for a whole year until we get settled on the island. Then we might look at buying a place of our own. Maybe Miss MacPhee might even sell us the cottage if we like it enough.'

Cammie let out an angry cry. 'You mean I'll have no home of my own any more! It's just not fair!'

'Why don't you live in the forest with the other fairies?' Rosie asked, puzzled.

Cammie almost choked on his reply. 'I'll have you know that I am *not* a fairy! I am a wee man, of the clan MacPherson, and just you remember that!'

'Wee men aren't quite the same as fairies, Rosie,' a soothing fairy voice explained, from behind her. 'Even though they do have fairy wings like us.'

'We do *not* have fairy wings!' Cammie interrupted angrily. 'It's you fairies who have *wee man* wings!' He whirled round and let out a dismayed gasp as he saw that the fairy who had spoken was Queen Mae herself. 'Why, Your Highness . . . I mean, Your Majesty . . . I didn't realize . . .'

Queen Mae ignored him and carried on talking to Rosie. 'You see, Rosie, there are lots of wee men living in houses where they're not likely to be spotted – empty holiday cottages or big houses where certain rooms aren't used much or in houses where there's an old person who doesn't see very well. There's a blind lady who lives across the other side of the loch and she's got six wee men living in her house with her, though she doesn't know it. They do all sorts of things to help her too, though she doesn't know that either. They're always washing her dishes for her and picking things up when she drops them.'

'But I thought most people couldn't see fairies anyway,' Rosie said.

'It's amazing the number of tourists who can't see us when we're standing right in front of their noses, that's true, but a fair few of the island people can see us all right,' Queen Mae replied. 'It's in their blood to see us wee folk. Some of them don't like us very much so they're the ones we have to hide away from.' She started to glance around. 'Now . . . where is Snowdrop? I thought I told her to look after you.'

'She *is* looking after me,' Rosie said quickly, not wanting Snowdrop to get into trouble. 'She's just gone for a stroll with one of the wee men, that's all.'

Just then the wee man in question came flying towards them carrying something large in his arms. As he got closer, they could see that what he was carrying was Snowdrop.

'What happened, Hughie?' Queen Mae asked, looking worried.

'She suddenly said she felt dizzy and then she fainted,' Hughie told them. 'She's come to now but she's still feeling very weak.'

'Lie her down over here and fetch some sphagnum moss straight away,' Queen Mae ordered. 'Snowdrop, my dear, try and tell me exactly what happened.'

Snowdrop murmured something that Rosie couldn't hear. Whatever it was, it made Queen Mae turn pale. 'We must get her home immediately,' she said. 'Cammie, I want you to take Rosie back across the loch in the boat and see her safely to her door. I'll take care of Snowdrop.'

'But what's wrong with her?' Rosie asked, suddenly feeling frightened. 'Is she sick?'

'I hope not,' replied Queen Mae. The other fairies had gathered round now and they were all looking scared as they whispered together. 'Hurry, now. No more questions. Hughie, can you carry her for me?'

'Of course,' Hughie said, and the two of them flew away together carrying Snowdrop, with all the other fairies following.

'Cammie do *you* know what's wrong with Snowdrop?' Rosie asked as they sat together in the boat on their way back across the loch. She was keeping an eye out for the dolphins and seals they had met on the way here, but there was no sign of them.

Cammie shook his head quickly, avoiding looking Rosie in the eye. He was frowning and he hadn't spoken once since they'd left the island.

Rosie was sure that he *did* know – and that he just didn't want to tell her.

As they reached the shore, Rosie glanced back for one last glimpse of the castle lit up by all the fairy lights, but it was already gone. All that Rosie could see now was the dark shape of the island in the middle of the loch, looking totally deserted.

The next morning Rosie was so sleepy she could hardly eat the toast and cereal her mother had put in front of her.

'Didn't you sleep well?' her mum asked, ruffling Rosie's fringe as she sat down at the table.

Rosie was about to make up an answer when she decided not to. After all, how could she expect her mother to start believing in the fairies if she never told her about them?

'I went to a fairy party last night on the island in the middle of the loch,' she said, in a rush. 'It was amazing, Mum! You know that ruined castle? Well, it wasn't a ruin any more, it was beautiful and it was all lit up with fairy lights and lanterns and all the fairies were dancing, only I couldn't join in because I was too big, but I watched. And I saw lots of seals . . . and even dolphins. And I met Queen Mae – she's the queen of the fairies – but the only thing that wasn't nice was that Snowdrop got dizzy and fainted at the end.'

'Really?' Her mother raised one eyebrow. 'Too much dancing I expect.'

'No, it was more serious than that. Queen Mae was really worried.' Rosie frowned. 'I hope Snowdrop's all right.'

'Rosie, listen to me a minute.' Her mother put down her mug of coffee and took Rosie's hand across the table. 'I'm getting worried about you.'

Rosie was puzzled. 'About *me*? Why?'

Her mum sighed. 'Because I keep hearing you talking to someone in your bedroom when there's nobody else there, and you've been playing a lot with the toys you used to play with when you were much younger – like your dolls' cot.' She paused. 'Rosie, I know it's very hard for you now that Dad and I have split up. And it's been difficult for you moving here because you haven't any friends yet and you have to spend so much time on your own. But that will all change when you start school after the holidays and meet some children your own age to play with. I think it's because you're feeling lonely at the moment that you've gone back to playing with your old toys and making up these imaginary friends. You used to have imaginary friends when you were little – do you remember?'

Rosie frowned. 'Snowdrop isn't like that. She isn't make-believe. She's real, Mum. And so are the wee men and Queen Mae and all the other fairies.'

'Rosie, listen,' her mother said firmly. 'It's natural to want to escape into an imaginary world when things are going wrong in real life. I do that myself a bit with my painting. But you're nine years old now and it's important to admit that the world you're making up inside your head is just that – a make-believe place you can escape to when things go wrong. Do you understand?'

'Mum, it's not make-believe!' Rosie protested. 'It's *real*! Ask old Flora if you don't believe me!'

'*Old Flora?* Rosie, I think you mean *Miss MacPhee*!'

'The fairies call her old Flora and she doesn't really mind. She can see them too. It's only you who can't.' Rosie left her breakfast and ran out of the cottage. It was no good. Her mum was *never* going to believe she was telling the truth!

She dodged round the side of the cottage as her mother opened the front door and called out her name. Rosie stayed put until her mum went back inside. Then, after inspecting the garden quickly for any sign of fairies, Rosie walked back past the front of the house, noticing as she did so that the front door wasn't shut properly. She could hear her mother's voice. She was on the telephone in the hallway.

'James, I'm really worried about her . . .'

Rosie stopped in her tracks. Mum was talking to her dad!

'She honestly seems to believe everything she says. It's as if she's retreated into an imaginary world or something and she won't let anybody in . . .' Her mother paused, listening for a minute or two. 'Yes, but, James . . . you remember when

she was four or five, you used to play that
game with her . . . making out there was a
wee man who lived in the corner, and you put
on that funny squeaky voice and made him
talk to her. You remember? Well, now she's
talking about seeing wee men here. And it
doesn't help that the old lady next door is as
nutty as a fruitcake and seems to be filling
her head full of fairy-stories too.'

Rosie listened, feeling surprised. *She* could-
n't remember her father making up any stories
about wee men when she was little. And Miss
MacPhee *wasn't* nutty! But still, it was amazing
that her parents actually seemed to be *talking*
to each other for once, not arguing.

Rosie was longing to see Snowdrop again but
for the rest of that day and all of the next,
there was no sign of her. In desperation, Rosie
left a chocolate on the window ledge for her
on the second night, but it was still there
when she woke up in the morning. Where
could Snowdrop be? Rosie couldn't believe
that she was all that sick. After all, the fairies
could easily make her better by mixing
together some sphagnum moss and some
fairy dust, couldn't they?

Rosie decided to leave a message for her friend up by the fairy forest. That way one of the fairies would be bound to spot it and take it to her. So that morning after breakfast, she took the big heart-shaped chocolate in purple foil that she had been saving for last because it was her favourite, and wrapped a note around it. On the outside of the note she printed:

TO SNOWDROP

and inside she wrote, in her neatest handwriting:

PLEASE COME AND SEE ME SOON!
LOVE ROSIE.

Rosie easily found the tree trunk beside the forest with the circle of little flowers round the outside. She left Snowdrop's chocolate on top, looking around to see if there were any fairies about, but today she couldn't see any. Still, Snowdrop was bound to get her message sooner or later and then Rosie was sure she would come and see her.

That night, after the cottage was in darkness and she was almost falling asleep, Rosie heard a gentle knocking on her window. She had left the window open so she wasn't surprised when a small figure flew inside and landed on the end of her bed. 'Snowdrop!' she called out excitedly.

But it wasn't Snowdrop. It was Cammie.

'Snowdrop asked me to thank you for the chocolate,' he said.

Rosie switched on her bedside lamp. 'Is she still poorly then?'

'Yes . . .' Cammie flew up to stand on the little bedside table where he looked into her face gravely. 'Rosie, I'm afraid you probably won't be seeing Snowdrop again. You see, she's very sick indeed.'

Rosie felt her stomach flip over. 'How do you mean? I'll see her when she gets better, won't I?'

Cammie turned his eyes downward. 'You see, there is one illness which fairies can get that is very serious indeed. We call it "the ending sickness".' He wiped his eyes with one of his lacy sleeves and muttered, 'It's terrible. . . just terrible . . .'

'But, what *is* the ending sickness?'

Cammie waved his hand at her dismissively. 'I'm not allowed to tell you that.'

'But if you told me, maybe I could help!'

Cammie shook his head. 'To explain the ending sickness, I'd have to tell you how a fairy is born, and if humans knew where fairies come from . . .' He trailed off, looking very uncomfortable.

Rosie was instantly full of more questions but, just then, there was a knock on her bedroom door. 'Rosie, who are you talking to in there?'

'You'd better go,' she whispered to Cammie as she saw the handle on her door start to turn.

Rosie's mum came into the room just as Cammie was flying out of the window. 'Are you all right, Rosie?'

'Yes, Mum,' Rosie said, quickly switching off the light.

Her mother said something else but Rosie hardly heard her. All she could think about now was Snowdrop.

Rosie found Flora sitting outside her cottage the next day with Angus on her lap. The old lady was talking softly to him and he was purring loudly as she fondled his ears.

'Miss MacPhee, I wanted to ask you something,' Rosie said, figuring that the best way to handle Flora was to get straight to the point.

'Oh, yes? Something about fairies, is it?' Flora had a twinkle in her eye.

'Miss MacPhee, have you ever heard of the "ending sickness"? It's something fairies get.'

Flora frowned. 'Aye, I've heard of it. There was a lovely little fairy used to come and see me years ago. Mimosa, her name was. One day she stopped coming. Next thing I heard was that she'd got the ending sickness. As far as I understand it, the ending sickness is the only way a fairy can die.'

'Oh, no.' Rosie felt her lip begin to tremble. 'It's just that . . . Snowdrop's . . . got it . . .' she whispered. And she burst into tears.

Miss MacPhee invited Rosie to sit down on her bench and tried to cheer her up by telling her she'd heard of one fairy who had recovered from the ending sickness, though she wasn't sure how. Hearing that gave Rosie a glimmer of hope and she made up her mind not to give up on Snowdrop.

She kept herself as busy as she could for the rest of the day and tried not to worry too much. Then, that evening, she sat up in bed with the window wide open and her bedroom light switched on so that if Cammie was about, he'd realize that she was awake and wanted to speak to him.

She didn't have to wait long. Cammie flew in through the window almost as soon as she'd gone to bed. 'Queen Mae wants to see you,' he said. 'She'll meet you outside in the garden when your mother's gone to sleep.'

'Is Snowdrop . . . ?' Rosie was petrified that Snowdrop had already died. After all, why else would the fairy queen want to speak to her in person?

'Queen Mae will wait for you in the garden,'

Cammie repeated firmly and he flew away again before she could ask anything more.

Rosie waited for what seemed like for ever for the light under her mother's bedroom door to disappear. Finally, after she had waited a bit longer to give her mum time to fall asleep, she tiptoed downstairs, dreading the news she was sure awaited her there.

She stepped out into the garden and spotted Queen Mae straight away. The moonlight caught her wings, making them shimmer as she flew over to the stone bird table in the middle of the grass in front of the cottage.

'How's . . . Snowdrop?' Rosie stammered, already afraid that she knew the answer.

But, to her relief, Queen Mae replied, 'She's sleeping now. She needs to sleep as much as she can to conserve her energy.'

'I know what the ending

sickness means,' Rosie said, quickly. 'Flora told me.'

Queen Mae nodded. 'Then you know how serious the situation is. And it's because of that that I'm going to ask for your help. I've discussed it with all the other fairies and we're agreed. You helped Snowdrop before, so we thought you might help her again.' She gazed at Rosie, her beautiful blue eyes looking very solemn. 'You see, Rosie, no fairy has ever told any human what I am about to tell you. Not even old Flora knows this – and she knows more about us than any of the other people on the island. Rosie, I'm going to tell you the biggest fairy secret of all! But you must promise never to repeat it to anyone else.'

Rosie murmured, 'I promise,' and held her breath, waiting to hear what was coming next.

'Fairies don't just appear out of nowhere,' Queen Mae began. 'When a fairy is made, it is for a very special reason – a reason connected with humans.' She lowered her voice to a whisper. 'What most humans don't know is that when a human child dies it doesn't just disappear into nothing. Whenever a little girl or boy dies anywhere in the world, a bundle of joy is left over. That joy is invisible to human eyes but a white dove collects it. The dove brings the bundle to the nearest fairy nursery where it empties it into a fairy crib, and our fairy nannies look after it until it changes from a bundle of joy into a newborn fairy.'

'WOW!' Rosie gasped. For a few moments she felt stunned. 'You mean . . . a new fairy is born . . . in place of any child who . . . dies?'

Queen Mae nodded. 'There is so much happy energy left over when a child dies, you see – all the energy that was going to be used up during that child's life. And it is that energy that goes into the making of a fairy.'

Rosie was silent for a few minutes, looking up at the stars, then back at Queen Mae, who was watching her with a gentle smile on her face.

'The white doves who bring us the bundles of joy are the only real link between humans and fairies,' the queen continued. 'They are the only ones who know which fairy came from which child. But they can never tell us, because if a fairy discovers the identity of her child then the magic breaks down and the fairy disappears for ever. So the white doves never tell any of the fairies where any of the bundles of joy come from . . . which is why *we* can't do anything to help any fairy who gets the ending sickness.'

'I don't understand,' Rosie said, lost now. 'Queen Mae, what *is* the ending sickness exactly? I mean, I know a fairy can die from it, but what causes it?'

'A fairy can live for a very long time,' Queen Mae explained. 'As long as the child the fairy came from is kept alive in a human's memory. But if the child is forgotten, the fairy will get the ending sickness and die.' Queen Mae paused. 'The person remembering doesn't have to have known the child themselves – they might just have been told about him or her. Some fairies live for hundreds of years because human families hand down memories of their loved ones from generation to generation.'

'So . . . you mean . . . the reason Snowdrop is sick is because no one is remembering her special child any more?' Rosie stammered.

Queen Mae nodded. 'That's right. And if you help us to change that, then we might be able to save Snowdrop.'

Rosie was still confused. 'But how can I help when we don't even know which child

Snowdrop came from? If the doves won't tell us, there isn't any way of finding out, is there?'

'The doves will never tell us fairies,' Queen Mae replied, giving her an intense look. 'But that doesn't mean they won't tell *you*.'

Rosie stared at the fairy queen.

Queen Mae held her gaze. '*Now* do you understand why I'm telling you all of this, Rosie? We have a bundle of joy being delivered at midday tomorrow. If you come to the forest then, you might be able to speak with the dove who brings it and find out who Snowdrop's child was.'

Rosie nodded slowly. Of course she would do anything she could to help Snowdrop. 'But how will I get a bird to talk to me?' She asked, frowning.

'Oh, don't worry about that,' Queen Mae replied. 'Just talk and it will understand you. These aren't ordinary doves. They live for a hundred years or more and there are only a few attached to each fairy village. The one who is coming tomorrow will remember whose child Snowdrop was. It will find a way of telling you if you ask it.'

'But even if I do find out, what will I do next?' Rosie asked.

'That's the easy bit,' Queen Mae said, brightening up. 'You just have to find as many people as possible who knew that child – and find a way of making them remember her again.'

'Right,' Rosie murmured, struggling not to frown. She didn't want to disappoint Queen Mae but, secretly, she didn't think that bit sounded very easy at all.

It was after nine o'clock when Rosie woke up the following morning, and her mother was already downstairs in the kitchen making breakfast. By the smell of it, she was cooking bacon, which must mean she was in a good mood. Her mother hardly ever bothered to make a cooked breakfast for them.

After Rosie had finished her bacon roll and got herself washed and dressed, she pottered about in her room for a while, tidying up and trying not to think about Snowdrop. At eleven o'clock she went downstairs and told her mother she was going for a walk up on the moor.

'I'll come with you, if you like,' her mum offered. 'Keep you company.'

But for once, that wasn't what Rosie

wanted. 'It's OK, Mum. I'd rather go by myself,' she said.

Her mother looked surprised and a little hurt but there was nothing Rosie could do about that. She *had* to make contact with the white dove – and she couldn't do that if her mum was around.

She walked up on to the moor and kept heading towards the forest, not really sure what she was going to do when she got there. When she reached the tree trunk where she had left the chocolate the day before, she sat down on it to wait. It was only half past eleven. Soon, she started to get a funny feeling inside, as if something magical was about to happen. Maybe the tree trunk would open up like a trapdoor, to reveal a secret passage or something, that would lead her into the centre of the forest. She tapped on top of the wood three times but nothing happened. She moved to sit on the ground so she could rest her back against the stump. The sun was very bright now and it hurt her eyes every time she stared up at the sky for any sign of a white bird. She closed her eyes for a while, beginning to feel sleepy as the heat got to her, then, as she opened her eyes to check her watch, she noticed a bird in the sky overhead. As it came closer, she saw that it was a white dove. Rosie stood up as it flew over her. It was carrying a small, white bundle in its beak, soaring high above the trees, heading towards the centre of the forest.

Rosie felt excited. She left the tree stump and began to walk among the trees. The further in she walked, the darker it became. She called out, 'Hello,' a few times, feeling sure that the centre of the forest must be where

the fairies lived, but all she heard was her own voice sounding spooky as it echoed back to her. The trees got closer and closer together and soon she couldn't tell which way she was walking any more. All she could make out when she looked up at the forest roof was blackness. It was dark underfoot as well and when she tripped up on a massive tree root, she decided to turn back.

And that was when she realized that she didn't know which direction led out of the forest. She *thought* she knew at first, so she kept walking, but instead of finding her way back, she kept coming up against more and more closely packed trees. Soon she was feeling really scared. What if she *never* found her way out of the forest again? Her mother didn't even know where she was. How was anyone ever going to find her?

Just as she felt like bursting into tears, she came to a tiny clearing, in the middle of which was another tree trunk. And perched on this tree trunk, as though it were waiting for her, was the white dove!

The bird's beak was empty now and as soon as it saw her, it flew off the tree stump and started to fly between the trees ahead of her, landing on a branch every now and again to look back, as if to check Rosie was following. Rosie easily kept the dove in sight as it flew at just the right speed to make sure it didn't lose her. She hurried after it, talking to it in the same way that Miss MacPhee talked to Angus, as if it could understand her perfectly even though it couldn't speak. '. . . so you see, I really need to know who Snowdrop's special child was if I'm going to help the fairies to save her. I won't tell *them* because I know I'm not allowed to, but if you tell me, I might be able to help . . .'

Suddenly she saw chinks of blue sky through the trees and then she was back at the forest edge, standing in the sunshine again.

'*Can* you talk?' she asked the bird, thinking that perhaps the fairies had worked their magic on it too, but the dove just continued to fly on ahead of her in the direction of the road. It sat waiting for her on top of the gate, flying off again as Rosie climbed over it. As Rosie started to cross the road towards Thistle Cottage, the dove started making loud cooing noises, flying wildly about her head, like a sheepdog trying to hustle a sheep that was heading in the wrong direction. It clearly wanted to lead her some place further.

Rosie followed the dove as it soared ahead of her along the single-track road and stopped at another gate some way along from Thistle Cottage. Rosie looked over into the field and recognized in the distance the old graveyard down by the loch. Judging from the ruins, there had been a church there too, long ago.

Rosie climbed over the gate and tramped across the grassy field to take a closer look. The graves were all facing the loch and they were all so old that none of them was tended any more. The white dove had settled on top of one of them. The bird didn't move as Rosie crouched down and pushed the long grass away from the front of the headstone where it was perched. The stone was covered in moss and ivy on one side and most of the writing was difficult to make out but it was easy to read the name inscribed at the top: *SARAH*. Rosie could just make out enough of the other words to tell that the grave belonged to a child who had died when she was seven years old. There was a date – *January 14th 1927* – and under the date were the names of Sarah's parents, *William and Anne McIver.*

The dove cocked its head downwards as if to draw her attention again to the name on the gravestone. Then it took off and went soaring away towards the loch.

'Thank you!' Rosie called out after it because she knew there could be only one reason why the dove had brought her here . . .

Sarah McIver must be Snowdrop's special child!

Rosie decided that the first thing she had to do was visit Flora again and see if she had known Sarah McIver. She went straight away.

Flora was sitting on the bench outside her cottage eating a bowl of lentil soup when Rosie walked down her driveway. Angus was crouched in the shade under the bench, eating what looked like a plate of kippers. Rosie reckoned that Miss MacPhee probably spent more time planning Angus's menu than she did her own.

'Have you heard any more about Snowdrop?' Flora asked, pausing between mouthfuls.

'Just that she's still really ill,' Rosie replied, wishing she could explain everything but knowing that she musn't. 'Miss McPhee, I was wondering if you knew anyone called

Sarah McIver when you were little. I found her grave just now in the old graveyard down by the loch and I worked out she'd be about the same age as you if she hadn't died. She died when she was seven.'

'Did she, indeed?' Flora started to eat her soup again. 'And how old is it that you think I am, then?'

Rosie blushed. 'Well, Sarah would have been eighty-two if she was still alive. I worked it out.'

'And you think I must be about that old too, do you?'

Rosie went even redder. 'Well . . . maybe not quite as old as that—' she began, but the old lady interrupted her.

'I'll be eighty years old next Saturday if you must know. What do you think of that, then?'

'Next Saturday?' Rosie was temporarily distracted. 'Are you having a party? When my grandad was eighty, we had a huge party for him! All his friends and family came to it.'

'Och, I haven't got any family – and not much in the way of friends either,' Flora said dismissively. 'I'll be having a quiet day here by myself with Angus. I expect I'll buy myself

85

a nice iced cake from the mobile shop when it visits on Friday.' She blew on a spoonful of soup. 'Now who was this person you wanted to know about? Sarah McIver, you say? I can't say I remember anyone by that name when I was growing up, but I do remember an *Annie* McIver. She was in my class in school. I was just thinking about her as a matter of fact. Saw her in the paper.' She picked up the newspaper that was lying on the bench and pointed to the section that listed Births, Deaths and Marriages. She jabbed her finger at an announcement in the Deaths column.

'Annie McIver,' Rosie read out loud. She looked at the date given. It was three days ago. The paragraph said that Annie McIver, aged seventy-nine, originally from Shee Village on the Isle of Skye, had died peacefully in her sleep in a nursing home in Glasgow.

Rosie frowned. Three days ago coincided with the fairy party when Snowdrop had first become unwell. Was Annie a relative of Sarah's? Had *she* been the one remembering her for all these years?

'Miss MacPhee, could Sarah have been Annie's sister?' Rosie asked. 'Were Annie's parents called William and Anne, do you remember?'

Flora shook her head. 'I'm sorry, my dear. I really can't remember that.'

If Sarah had been Annie's sister, and her only one, then it made sense that, with Annie gone, there would be nobody left who remembered Sarah. After all, she had died seventy-five years ago, hadn't she? It was unlikely that anyone other than close family would still be thinking about someone after all that time. But some of the other old people from the village must have known her too, once upon a time. Some of them must have played with her as children.

'Could you take me to see some of the other old people who live here?' Rosie asked. 'I'd really like to ask them if they knew Sarah.'

Flora frowned. 'I've no cause to be visiting any folk round here, thank you very much. They've all got their own lives now, with children, most of them, and grandchildren too. I've nothing to say to any of them any more.'

Rosie was only half listening. An idea about how to help Snowdrop had come to her while Flora was talking. 'Why don't you have a birthday party next week and invite all the other old people in the village? You could hire out the village hall. Mum asked about it because she was thinking she might have an exhibition of her paintings there one evening. It's owned by the church and Mum found out that they let people have it for free if they can't afford to pay anything.'

Miss MacPhee had a pink spot on each cheek now. She had stopped eating her soup. 'I am not a charity case, Rosie Macleod!' she snapped. 'And if I wanted a party– which I don't – I'd organize it myself. Now, I think you'd

better be getting back to your mother. I'm sure she must be wondering where you are.'

'I'm sorry,' Rosie began in a small voice. 'I didn't mean . . .'

But Flora was already standing up and making a shooing motion at her.

Rosie wished she could have told her about Snowdrop and the *real* reason she wanted to get all the old people in the village together again. She supposed she could always organize a birthday party for Flora in any case, without the old lady knowing, and tell everyone it was going to be a surprise party like the one they'd had for her grandad. Somehow, Rosie didn't think Flora would be as pleased as her grandad had been, but still . . . time was running out. And Rosie couldn't think of any other way to help Snowdrop.

It turned out that the most helpful person, once she'd told him her plan, was Cammie. She couldn't tell Cammie about Sarah McIver but she could tell him that she knew who Snowdrop's child had been and that, although Flora couldn't remember her, there was a chance that if they got all the old people in the village together then *someone* would. And Cammie agreed that the best way to get a whole lot of people together at once was to throw a party.

Cammie liked the idea of making it a surprise party for Flora's birthday. 'She'll go mental when she finds out,' he grinned, as if that was going to make it all the more enjoyable.

'I hope she's not too angry,' Rosie said, frowning. 'Though as long as we get everyone together, that's the important thing for Snowdrop.'

'I shouldn't worry. I bet old grumpy drawers won't even come,' Cammie said.

Rosie giggled. 'She'd kill you if she heard you call her that!'

'Och, she'd have to catch me first and you can't catch a MacPherson if he's a mind not to be caught!' Cammie did a little jig as if to show off how nimble-footed he was. 'I can deliver the invitations if you like. I'll get all my brothers to help.'

'How many brothers have you got?' Rosie asked.

'Nine that I know of.' He started to count them on his fingers. 'Calum, Willie, Big

Dougal, Jimmy, Murdo, Ewan, Fraser, Gordon and Wee Dougal. And there are many more MacPhersons than that. I've thirty-two cousins . . .' He started to count on his fingers again. 'Hamish, Andrew, Stuart—'

'I'm glad you're such a big family,' Rosie interrupted him, before he could list them all. 'Because we'll need lots of help getting the invitations delivered before Saturday. I can make them but you'll need to see they get put in the right letter boxes. Will you be able to do that?'

'Of course. We'll sprinkle some fairy dust on them too if you like, just to make sure people are in the mood for a party when they open them up. There's a few folk who might not go otherwise. Old Flora isn't exactly the most popular person hereabouts.'

'Don't people like her, then?' Rosie asked, surprised.

'They think she's a bit eccentric, that's all,' Cammie said, 'the way she hardly ever leaves her house and never speaks to anyone save the English foreigners like you who rent out Thistle Cottage.'

'I'm not an English foreigner!' Rosie said crossly. 'My mum's Scottish and my dad is half-Scottish, so I'm nearly all Scottish even though I was born in England.'

'Sorry! Sorry!' Cammie grinned. 'I just keep thinking of you as foreign because of that funny English way you speak, that's all. Never mind. I dare say, you'll start speaking normally when you've lived here a while longer.'

'Stop being horrible!' Rosie snapped.

'You're the one who's horrible,' Cammie said, looking a bit cross himself as he flew over to inspect the top shelf in the alcove where he had previously been living. 'Turning me out of my home and leaving me with no place to stay!'

'Can't you find another cottage?' Rosie asked.

Cammie scowled. 'Aye, but it wouldn't be as cosy as the place I've got here. I don't suppose you've looked behind those books on the top shelf, have you?'

Rosie shook her head. 'Why?' she asked. 'What's there?'

'My home, that's what. I thought you were going to leave again after the summer so I just left everything there. You can take a peek if you like.'

Rosie dragged her bedroom chair over to the shelved alcove and stood on it. Now that she could reach the shelf Cammie was talking about, she pulled out a few of the books and found that the shelf behind them went back a surprisingly long way. And hidden behind the row of dusty books was a doll-sized room, just big enough to house a wee man. At one end of the shelf was a soft bed made of dry, springy moss, with a white handkerchief spread over it to make a cover. Next to the bed was a toadstool table with a smaller toadstool seat

next to it. Hanging on the wall above the table was a miniature portrait of a wee man dancing in full Highland dress, which Cammie proudly explained was a picture of him doing the Highland fling. At the other end of the shelf from the bed there was a pink Barbie doll's wardrobe and a chest of drawers made out of matchboxes.

'I picked that up at a jumble sale,' Cammie told her, pointing at the wardrobe proudly. 'It's bonnie, don't you think?'

Rosie looked at him. 'Cammie . . . ' She paused. 'Listen, I don't mind if you want to move back in here. My mum never looks behind those books so she'd never find out.'

'Really?' Cammie looked delighted.

Rosie nodded.

'Well . . .' Cammie suddenly changed his grin to a thoughtful frown, like he at least wanted to go through the motions of carefully considering Rosie's offer. 'I suppose it *might* suit me, so long as you promise not to peek at me when I'm getting undressed or anything like that.'

'Of course I wouldn't!' Rosie protested.

'And as long as you don't snore. I can't abide that when I'm trying to get to sleep.'

'I don't *think* I snore,' Rosie said, frowning. 'Cammie, you don't have to move back in if you don't want to. I just thought—'

'I'll give it a try,' Cammie said quickly. 'I

suppose I can wear my earplugs if you're too noisy. I'll go and fetch my things back and, while I'm about it, I'll ask some of the other wee men to help me make a list of the old folk round here. It shouldn't be difficult since most of us are living in their cottages.'

'Great!' Rosie smiled. 'I'll get some paper and make out the invitations so they'll be ready when you get back.'

Rosie wrote in big letters:

PARTY INVITATION!!!
YOU ARE INVITED TO A SURPRISE PARTY
FOR MISS FLORA MACPHEE'S 80th BIRTHDAY!

She used a red pen to make the letters, then drew gold squiggles underneath with the special pen her mother always used to write on birthday cards. Next she added the place – the town hall – and the time and date – seven o'clock in the evening next Saturday. Then she printed RSVP with her own name and telephone number beside it. All she had to do now was ask her mother to book the hall.

When Cammie came back much later, balancing his matchbox-suitcase on his head, he told her she should make out twenty invitations. 'I've talked to the other wee men and that's all the folk we can think of over the age of seventy-five who live near enough to come,' he said. 'I don't know that they were all brought up here, but some of them must have been.'

'That's fine,' Rosie said. 'All we need is a few who remember Sa—' She stopped herself quickly. She had been about to say Sarah's name and she knew she wasn't meant to tell it to Cammie. 'No fairy or wee man will be able to come to the party,' Rosie reminded him. 'Because after the party starts, I'm going to have to say the name of Snowdrop's child out loud.'

'Don't worry. We won't feel like going to a party, anyway,' Cammie said grimly. 'We're all too worried about Snowdrop. She's getting weaker every day. You know, if our plan doesn't work, she'll only have a few days left.'

Rosie looked down at the fairy flower bracelet that she still wore on her wrist, the one Snowdrop had made for her. 'It *will* work,' she said, crossing her fingers tightly. 'It's *got* to!'

The invitations had all been sent out and Cammie's fairy dust must have worked because nearly everyone who had received an invitation had telephoned Rosie's mum to say they would be coming. Her mother had booked the church hall and she had invited Reverend Mackay and his wife to the party too. He was nearing retirement and had three sisters, all older than him, the eldest of whom had been in Flora's class at school. So Rosie made sure they invited the minister's sisters to the party as well, and Reverend MacKay thought they would come, even though they lived on different parts of the island now.

'I still can't believe that Miss MacPhee told you she wished someone would throw a party for her,' her mum said, for the tenth time, as she put down the phone after taking a call from yet another person who was accepting their invitation. 'Nobody you've invited can, either. They say they always thought she didn't want anything to do with anybody.'

Rosie crossed her fingers behind her back and reminded herself that this was only a white lie to save Snowdrop. 'Well, she does.'

Her mother sighed. 'I hope you're right, Rosie. I can't say Miss MacPhee has ever struck me as the type of person who'd relish the idea of a party. Maybe I should check with her first.'

'No, Mum. It'll spoil the surprise,' Rosie protested.

'Well . . .' Her mother still looked uncertain.

'Please, Mum . . .' Rosie begged.

'Well, I suppose it can't really do any harm,' her mum sighed. 'Reverend Mackay seems to think it's a good idea and his wife is going to help me get the hall ready.'

She didn't have time to say any more because the phone rang again. This time, though, it wasn't someone accepting a party invitation. It was Rosie's dad. He was phoning to let them know that he was coming to see them this weekend!

Rosie was really excited. 'That means Dad can come to the party,' she beamed, after they put down the phone.

Her mum was smiling too, until Rosie added, breathlessly, 'I can't believe he's really going to be here! On Sunday we can go out in Miss MacPhee's boat . . . all three of us! We can show Dad the seals!'

'Rosie, you do realize that Dad is coming to spend time with *you*, don't you?' Her mother said slowly. 'I mean . . . Dad and I are still friends but our marriage is over.'

Rosie saw her mother's worried look. 'It's OK, Mum,' she said softly. 'I know that.' Because she did know it. Most of the time.

Her mum stared at her for a moment or two. 'I'm sorry, darling,' she sighed, then she pulled her close and gave her a hug.

That night Rosie couldn't sleep. Cammie hadn't got back yet from visiting Snowdrop in the fairy forest and Rosie was getting worried. Why was he taking so long?

Just as she was about to get up for the

tenth time to look out of the window, Cammie flew in through the bedroom door. 'Thought I'd come in down the chimney in the living room for a change,' he explained, dusting some soot from his kilt and sneezing loudly.

'How's Snowdrop?' Rosie asked anxiously.

'Not good, I'm afraid. Queen Mae is looking after her. She's very weak now. She's resting on the Queen's special rose-petal bed which makes you have lovely dreams when you sleep on it.'

'What does Queen Mae think about our idea?' Rosie asked. 'Does she think it'll work?'

'She says it might. But because Snowdrop is *so* sick now, she thinks it'll take more than just one person remembering. She thinks you'll have to get lots of people all remembering Snowdrop's child at once.'

'Oh, dear,' Rosie sighed. 'I hope I can do that.'

'I *know* you can do it,' Cammie replied, flying over to the mirror and frowning at his sooty face. 'And when a MacPherson knows a thing, he's always right!' He looked back at Rosie. 'All the fairies are counting on you, Rosie. You can't let us down now.'

Rosie swallowed. She wanted to say something but found that she couldn't make any words come out. Her throat felt like it had closed over. Finally she managed to say, in a hoarse voice, 'I wish I didn't have to do this on my own. I wish Mum believed me about the fairies.'

Cammie looked at her softly. His voice was much gentler as he said, 'She can't help not believing. Anyway, it's because she *doesn't* believe that she's got all worried about you and phoned up your dad. And that's probably why he's decided to visit you this weekend. He must care about you a lot to come all this way, don't you think?'

Rosie nodded, slowly. No matter what had happened between her mum and dad, her dad *did* care about her. And she gave Cammie a smile for reminding her of that.

Rosie was so busy planning ahead for the party that she kept forgetting that her dad was coming and every time she remembered, she couldn't help smiling again, even though she was still really worried about Snowdrop.

She felt very excited as she waited for him

to arrive on Friday afternoon. He had flown as far as Inverness, then hired a car to drive from Inverness over the road-bridge to Skye.

'He's here!' Rosie shouted upstairs to her mother, as she spotted him pull into their driveway from the kitchen window. Her mum had changed twice today already and was now upstairs touching up her make-up. Rosie's mother hadn't worn make-up since they'd arrived on the island and Rosie was surprised that she was going to so much trouble just because her dad was coming to stay. Secretly she hoped it might mean that her mum was having good feelings about her dad, despite what she'd said about them never getting back together again. After all, there was always a chance, wasn't there?

'Rosie!' Her dad flung open the car door and lifted her up. They hugged for several minutes before he asked, 'Where's your mother?'

That was good as well, Rosie thought. That her dad had asked about her straight away. She felt a bit cross with her mum, though. Why hadn't she come out to greet him?

'She's in the house getting ready,' Rosie said, doing her best to make it clear that her mother *had* prepared for his arrival. 'Come on.'

Her mum met them in the hallway looking pretty but nervous, Rosie thought. Her parents went to kiss each other, but only on the cheek. When she was younger, her parents had always kissed and hugged for ages whenever one of them had been away. Rosie used to think it was soppy. Now she'd give anything to see them act like that again.

'I've brought my kilt for this party tomorrow night, Rosie,' her dad said as he brought his bags into the house. 'You won't be embarrassed by my hairy legs, will you?'

'Don't be silly! Anyway, Cammie's got much hairier legs than you!'

'Cammie?'

'I'm sure Rosie will tell you all about Cammie and the other fairies later,' her mother said, giving him an I-told-you-so look.

Rosie saw the look and wished she hadn't said anything. Just as her dad started to reply, his mobile phone went off.

'Oh, no,' her mum scowled. 'Couldn't you leave that thing at home for once?'

Her dad explained that he had an important court case coming up and that he'd
promised to remain contactable while he
was here.

'And what about the promise you made to
Rosie?' her mother said, sharply. 'You prom-
ised to spend your time with *her* this weekend.
Remember?'

'It's OK, Mum,' Rosie said quickly, starting
to feel all churny inside like she always used to
when her parents argued in front of her.

'Look, I'll only be a minute!' her dad said,
turning away to speak into his mobile.

Rosie's mum rolled her eyes and stomped
into the kitchen. That had happened a lot
when they lived in London – her mum rolling
her eyes like that and going off in a bad mood
after something Dad had done. Rosie used to
feel like she was piggy in the middle all the
time, unable to decide whether to follow her
mum or stay with her dad. At least she'd been
able to leave that feeling behind when they'd
left London.

As Rosie waited for her dad to come off
his mobile she realized that something else
had changed. In London, whenever her mum
and dad had argued, she had always been

scared. She'd been scared in case they were going to split up. Now, because that had already happened, there was nothing to be afraid of any more. And, in a funny kind of way, that felt better.

After tea, Rosie's mum suggested that Rosie take her father to see some of the country-side around the cottage. So Rosie took him down to the loch, then up on to the moor where she showed him the special tree stump beside the forest with the flowers round the outside. She also showed him the flower bracelet Snowdrop had made for her. She knew he didn't believe her about the fairies but she was so happy he was there that she didn't really care.

It was later that night that everything started to go wrong.

Rosie went downstairs to fetch a glass of water from the kitchen and paused in the hall. She could hear her parents discussing her as they set up her dad's camp bed in the living room.

'She's always had a very active imagina-tion, Maggie,' her father was saying. 'You always used to see that as a good thing.'

'When she was younger, yes. Then she was doing the usual thing of making up imaginary friends. This is different. She seems to really *believe* in these fairies. I'm worried about her, James. I'm worried this is some sort of weird reaction to us breaking up. Maybe I did the wrong thing moving her up here. I *thought* she'd be happy here. I thought it would be a wonderful place for her to grow up . . .'

Before Rosie's dad could answer, his mobile phone started ringing again.

Rosie heard her father answer the call, then she heard his voice getting more and more tense until he said, 'Look, are you sure I need to be there?' He spoke to whoever it was for several more minutes before ringing off. 'I'm sorry, Maggie. They've had to call an emergency meeting at work tomorrow. They're flying someone else in from New York and they need me to be there too. I'll have to leave first thing in the morning.'

'Oh, James!' Rosie's mum sounded tired and on the verge of tears.

Rosie felt as if someone had kicked her in the stomach. She couldn't believe it. Dad couldn't be leaving again tomorrow – he just couldn't!

At that moment, she spotted Cammie sitting on the stairs, an orange flannel wrapped round him like a towel and his red hair sticking up in the air. He must have been listening too. Now he looked very determined. Before Rosie could stop him, he had flown right past her into the living room. A few seconds later her father sneezed loudly. Cammie came back out into the hall looking very pleased with himself. He winked at Rosie and ignored her whispered questions as he flew over her head back upstairs.

By the time Rosie had followed him to her bedroom, he had disappeared behind the books on the top shelf. And when she called out his name, all she got in response was a chuckle and a muffled, 'Fairy dust has *so* many uses!'

11

'Cammie, what have you done to him?' Rosie demanded as soon as she got back to her room after breakfast the following morning. Her father wasn't going back to London today after all. He couldn't because his face was covered in bright red spots.

'Och, he'll be back to normal by tonight,' Cammie said from behind the books on his shelf. 'I thought I'd see to it that he came to the party after all. That's what you wanted, wasn't it?'

'Yes, but—'

'Good!' Cammie's orange hair appeared above the books and his green eyes looked at her mischievously. 'Now we'd better go and visit old Flora and treat *her* to a bit of fairy dust too. That might get her in the mood for going to the party!'

But when they knocked on Flora's door and wished her a happy birthday, the old lady scowled. Cammie was sitting on Rosie's shoulder muttering to himself and rubbing his fingertips together in a mysterious manner.

'You keep that fairy dust away from me, you wee rascal!' Flora snapped, slamming the door in their faces before Rosie had even had a chance to speak.

They knocked again but there was no reply. 'It's no good,' Cammie sighed. 'And old Flora won't come to the party of her own free will. The last time she went to a party it was her own engagement party and that was fifty years ago.'

'Engagement party?' Rosie said. 'But she's never been married, has she?'

'No, and that's the reason she doesn't like parties. Her husband-to-be didn't turn up that day. He sent a message that he'd changed his mind about the wedding and was going off to live on the mainland instead. Some folk say that old Flora never got over it. She kept herself shut away after that and people soon stopped trying to visit because she never opened the door to them.'

'Poor Miss MacPhee,' Rosie said. She

couldn't imagine how horrible it must be to have that happen to you at your own engagement party. Rosie wondered what Flora had done after that. She must have felt really lonely. No wonder she always made such a fuss of Angus. Angus was her family really – and in a funny way, Rosie suddenly thought, so were the fairies.

As Cammie flew off to see Snowdrop, Rosie walked slowly back to Thistle Cottage, trying to think of another way to persuade Flora to come to the party.

That afternoon Rosie helped her mother and Mrs Mackay get the hall ready while her father stayed at home, still covered in spots. They put up the decorations her mother had made and blew up lots of brightly coloured balloons which they pinned to the wooden beams that ran across the ceiling. They laid out the party drinks and some of the food and later on Mrs Mackay was going to bring sandwiches and trifle and a big birth-day cake.

'Have you told Flora about the party, yet?' Mrs MacKay asked when they had finished getting everything ready.

Rosie's mum shook her head. 'Rosie and I will go round and tell her now, I think. Give her some time to get ready.'

Just then, Rosie's dad appeared in the doorway, dressed in his kilt. 'James!' her mum gasped. 'Shouldn't you be . . . ?' She stopped short as she saw that his spots were all gone.

'I feel fine now,' he replied, smiling. 'Must have been some kind of allergy or something. I reckon I'll be fit enough to come to this party tonight after all.'

'Dad, that's brilliant!' Rosie beamed, rushing over to give him a hug.

'You certainly *look* fine!' Mrs MacKay said, giving Rosie's mum a wink. 'You know, there's something about a bonnie man in a kilt that makes a lady go a bit weak at the knees, even when you're as old as I am. I reckon you should get your dad to ask Miss McPhee to the party, Rosie. If I know her, she's more likely to give in if *he* asks her.'

So that's what they did. Rosie took her

dad round to visit Miss MacPhee, who was a bit wary of him at first but then, to Rosie's amazement, she actually invited them inside her cottage. She made a pot of tea and they sat in her big old-fashioned kitchen chatting about the island and the wildlife, and Rosie's dad told Miss MacPhee about the huge ginger cat he'd had as a boy who had been *nearly* as handsome as Angus.

Finally, her dad took old Flora's hand and asked, very politely, 'Miss McPhee, the real reason for this visit is to ask if you'd do me the honour of accompanying me to a very special occasion tonight. You see . . . Rosie has organized a party for your birthday!'

'I beg your pardon?' Miss MacPhee looked astounded.

'She wanted it to be a surprise. A lot of the people in the village are coming and so is the Reverend Mackay and his wife and all three of his sisters. Everyone wants to celebrate your eightieth birthday with you. Please come!'

'They do?' Flora looked even more astounded. Then she scowled. 'They want to see what I look like after all these years, more likely.'

'Mrs MacKay has made this enormous birthday cake with pink icing and it's got your name written on it in blue icing and—' Rosie began, but Flora interrupted her.

'The Reverend's sisters you say? His eldest sister . . . Susan . . . was my best friend at school. Haven't seen her in years.'

'Well, you can see her again tonight. And she'll get to see you . . . making your entrance on my arm . . . *if* you'll allow me to escort you there.' Rosie's dad was smiling broadly.

Flora laughed. 'You are a charmer, aren't you?' She looked at Rosie. 'I suppose *you'd* be disappointed if I didn't come along and blow out my candles and all that rubbish, wouldn't you?'

'Yes,' Rosie nodded. 'You've got to come, Miss McPhee! Please!'

'All right, all right,' Flora grunted. 'Perhaps I will make an exception this time. I've still got the dress I bought for my last party so I suppose I may as well get some use out of it.'

As they left Flora's cottage, Rosie whispered to her dad, 'Cammie said the last party she went to was *fifty* years ago!'

Her dad laughed. 'Well, if Cammie's

right . . . and wee men usually are, I expect . . . let's just pray that it still fits her!' He winked at her and Rosie couldn't tell whether he was teasing or whether maybe . . . just maybe . . . he did believe her just a little bit about Cammie and the fairies, after all.

Cammie flew in through the window of Rosie's bedroom just as she was zipping up her own dress for the party. It was pink with sparkly sequins down the back and she had shiny shoes to go with it.

Cammie landed with a small thud on her bed and sat there, resting his chin in his hands, looking worried. 'Rosie, I think you should know, Snowdrop is very weak now.' His voice trembled a little as he added, 'She's about to fade away – you can see it starting. She won't be able to last the night.'

'Yes, she will!' Rosie said fiercely. She was feeling determined now. 'As soon as the party begins I'm going to start them off remembering the old days and then one of them's bound to remember Sa—' She stopped abruptly, just before saying Sarah's name. 'Look, you'd better leave now. Just come and tell me as soon as Snowdrop starts to get better . . . or if she . . .' She swallowed. She didn't want to say the awful thing that was on her mind out loud.

She watched her friend fly off into the night. If Snowdrop was going to get well again, it was up to Rosie to make their plan work. The guests at Flora's party *had* to remember Sarah McIver and they had to start talking about her. And the more they remembered and the more they talked, then the better chance Snowdrop had of recovering.

Rosie's mum drove them to the hall, with Flora sitting in the front of the car huddled up in a big cream shawl that covered most of her dress. Rosie sat beside her father in the back seat, feeling nervous. What if nobody remembered Sarah? What would she do then?

Rosie and her mum entered the hall first and smiled at the little groups of old people who were standing around drinking wine and chatting. Everybody stopped talking as Flora walked in on the arm of Rosie's dad. She had removed her shawl to reveal a stunning, dark blue, beaded dress. Rosie couldn't believe that it was fifty years old!

Everyone called out, 'HAPPY BIRTH-DAY!' and Reverend MacKay popped open a bottle of champagne and soon everyone was gathering around Flora asking her how she was and wishing her many happy returns and admiring her dress. To Rosie's amazement, Flora took one look at all her old friends and neighbours and started to cry.

'She's crying because she's happy, not because she's sad,' Mrs MacKay whispered in Rosie's ear. 'She never expected that we all still cared about her, that's all.'

Rosie sort of understood what Mrs MacKay meant. She knew people cried sometimes for happy reasons as well as sad ones. Her dad had cried when she was born, her mother had said, just because he was so happy. But she couldn't imagine what it was like to think nobody cared about you and then discover that they did.

Flora had spotted her old friend Susan and had gone over to speak to her. The two old ladies were standing looking at each other awkwardly, as if they didn't know where to begin after all this time, and Rosie decided that it was time to move in.

'Miss MacPhee, you know how I asked if you knew Sarah McIver . . . ?' Rosie spoke so loudly that everyone nearby could hear her too. 'Well, does anybody else here remember her, do you think? I think she might have been Annie's sister.'

Susan turned to look at Rosie. 'I remember *Annie* McIver well enough,' she said. 'She had a sister a couple of years older, I think, who died when we were children, but I don't think she was called Sarah. What was her name, now . . . ?' She beckoned to a white-haired old lady sitting sipping sherry in the corner. 'Morag, what was the name of the older McIver girl? The one who died that winter when everyone went down with the pneumonia? It wasn't Sarah, was it?'

The old lady called Morag stood up and

came over to them, carefully holding her sherry glass in both hands so that it didn't spill. 'No. It wasn't Sarah. We lived two houses along from the McIvers. I remember Annie used to talk about her. She was called . . . What was it? Susie . . . ? Katie . . . ?'

'*Sadie!*' a crackly voice called out, from a wheelchair parked beside the table.

'Sadie!' Morag exclaimed. 'That was it!'

The old lady in the wheelchair was waving

for Rosie to go over to her. 'I'm Miss MacIntyre,' she said hoarsely. 'I used to be Flora's teacher at the village school when *she* was your age.'

'*Flora's* teacher?' Rosie asked, as she hastily tried to calculate ages in her head.

'That's right. I'll be a hundred next year – the oldest person on the island!'

'Wow!' Rosie said. She had never met anyone as old as that before.

'So you want to know about Sadie McIver, do you?' Miss MacIntyre asked.

'Not Sadie . . . *Sarah* . . .' Rosie replied, frowning, but Miss MacIntyre just carried on smiling.

'Sarah was her proper name, right enough, but everyone called her Sadie. I haven't thought about that little girl in years. A bright little thing she was. One of my best pupils. I remember she was a little chatterbox. Always telling stories about the fairies and coming and showing me the presents they gave her. And such pretty blue eyes and golden hair. I remember once she found out it was my birthday and she brought me a bunch of snowdrops. I always remember how they lasted for weeks. Snowdrops don't usually last long after you pick them. She told me they were sprinkled with—'

'Fairy dust,' Rosie interrupted breathlessly.

All the old people were gathering round now.

'Aye, *I* remember those snowdrops,' an elderly man joined in. 'I remember I teased Sadie about them – about sucking up to the teacher! Gave me a right clout on the nose she did. Sadie McIver. I'd forgotten all about her. Sparky little thing, she was.'

Another old lady had joined them. 'You're not talking about wee Sadie who used to play with my brother, are you? She was a lively one! She'd completely slipped my mind but, do you know . . . I think I might have a photograph of her and our Cammie at home somewhere.'

'*Cammie?*' Rosie repeated, not sure that she had heard right.

'Aye . . . Sadie and my wee brother, Cameron, were the same age and they used to get up to all sorts of mischief together. They both took ill with the pneumonia that winter and they died within a few days of each other. I remember my mother telling me our

120

Cammie wouldn't be lonely up in heaven because he'd have his wee friend, Sadie, there to play with him . . .' She sighed, a little sadly.

Rosie's head felt like it was spinning. 'Excuse me, but is your name . . . ?'

'Mrs Bell, I am now,' the old lady said. 'But Lorna MacPherson, I was, before I married.'

'Then your brother was Cammie MacPherson!' Rosie gasped.

'That's right, lass. Only seven when he died. He didn't live long but I'll never forget him. Full of energy he was. And always laughing.'

Rosie closed her eyes, feeling even more dizzy. Not only had she discovered Snowdrop's special child, she had found Cammie's as well.

All around her the old people were talking about children they had known in the past when they were just children themselves. They were remembering their own brothers and sisters as well as the McIver sisters and other childhood friends who they hadn't thought about in years. The fiddle music that Reverend MacKay had been playing seemed to be getting louder and the chattering voices seemed to be getting further away. All the bright colours of the streamers and balloons and people's clothes seemed to be blurring into one another in front of Rosie's eyes. And the next thing she knew, she was lying on the floor with her mother and father leaning over her and Mrs MacKay standing behind, suggesting that maybe she'd fainted because of all the excitement.

'Or maybe she's coming down with something,' her mum said, anxiously. 'I think I'll take her home, James. You stay here and keep Miss MacPhee company.'

'I don't think Miss McPhee needs my company any more,' her dad said, pointing to where Flora was deep in conversation with three old ladies and an old gentleman who was fussing around her, offering her champagne and trifle. 'Why don't we *all* go home.'

So Rosie's parents asked Reverend MacKay if he would bring Flora home at the end of the evening, then they drove back to Thistle Cottage where Rosie's mother helped her out of her clothes and into bed.

After her mother had closed the door, Rosie lay very still, waiting. Presently, there was movement behind the curtains.

Rosie sat up abruptly. 'Snowdrop?' She

hardly dared to breathe.

It was Cammie. 'You did it, Rosie,' he grinned, flying over from the window and landing on her bed. 'Snowdrop's better. She's getting stronger by the minute. She wants you to come and visit her in the fairy forest tomorrow but she's got to ask Queen Mae first. I'm going back now because we're having our own party to celebrate, but if Queen Mae says yes, I'll be back tomorrow night to collect you.' He flew back to the window ledge and turned round again. 'By the way,' he added, grinning even more, 'I was wrong. You children are just as good friends to us now as you were in the old days!'

And before Rosie could reply, he was gone.

Before Rosie could see Snowdrop again, she had to say goodbye to her father. Rosie couldn't help feeling sad as her dad hugged her before getting into his car the following day. His visit had passed so quickly. He had promised to come and see her again soon, but he couldn't say exactly when and it was not knowing exactly when that made Rosie's insides feel all churny. Her mum tried to cheer her up as they stood at the gate together but Rosie couldn't stop a tear rolling down her cheek as she watched his car disappear from view.

When she went back to her bedroom she found Cammie waiting for her. As soon as he saw her he did an excited jig on her bed. 'Queen Mae says I'm allowed to bring you right into the middle of the forest and show you where the fairies live!' he announced. 'She's given me some special fairy dust to use. It's in here.' He tapped the leather pouch he had fastened to his belt.

'Really?' Now Rosie felt a bit better. 'When can we go?'

'Straight away. Queen Mae is expecting us.'

Rosie called out to her mother that she was going outside for a walk, then she hurried after Cammie who was already halfway up the drive.

Cammie led her across the moor towards the forest, pausing when they got to the tree stump with the flowers round the outside. 'From now on,' he said, making his voice sound very important, 'you must only tread where I sprinkle the fairy dust.'

Rosie ended up following him along much the same route as she had taken before. This time, though, she took care only to stand on the path of golden dust that Cammie was laying for her. She felt a funny tingling sensation all over her body as she walked, but it wasn't unpleasant and it didn't feel as if anything very special was happening to her as she followed him.

'You'd better close your eyes now,'

Cammie said, as the trees became denser.

'But I'll bump into the trees!'

'No, you won't. Just close your eyes and keep walking. The fairy dust will keep you on the right path.'

So Rosie did as Cammie told her, stepping forward warily at first, but then walking more confidently as she realized that the fairy dust path seemed to be leading her safely ahead in the same way a guide dog would lead a blind person. She couldn't even feel herself brushing against the trees that she knew must be there beside her, and all the time Cammie

was whistling a tune so that she knew he was still with her.

'You can open your eyes now,' Cammie eventually said.

She found that she was surrounded by giant tree trunks, much broader than any she had ever seen before. And when Cammie appeared through a space in the trees, he had grown in size so that he was now the same size as Rosie herself!

'I don't understand,' Rosie gasped, as he walked towards her. 'Where am I? And how did you make yourself that *big*?'

Cammie chuckled. 'I'm the same size as I always was,' he said. '*You're* the one who's changed. You're the same size as a fairy now.'

'What?' Rosie couldn't believe it.

'Come on,' Cammie grinned at her. 'The others are waiting.' He opened a door in a nearby tree and beckoned her to follow him inside.

Rosie stepped through the door and found herself in a hollowed-out tree trunk which went up and up so far that Rosie couldn't see the top.

'Just take hold of my hand and we'll fly up together,' Cammie said. Then, with Rosie's hand in his, he took off, flapping his wings energetically to propel them both upwards.

Soon Rosie could see sunlight above her and she found herself emerging from the darkness into an open grassy area which turned out to be some sort of village green. All around the green were little wooden houses with flowers growing round the doors. Fairies the same size as Rosie fluttered about, watering their window boxes and chatting with each other.

'Wow!' Rosie gasped.

They were standing beside a village well in the middle of the lawn. It was made of pink and purple bricks and a shiny gold bucket dangled from a chain attached to its little painted roof.

'We just flew out of there,' Cammie explained. 'The well is the only entrance to the village. It leads down into that tree trunk passage. At night the bucket glows in the dark and lights up the whole tunnel.'

Rosie stared in amazement at the well.

Some of the fairies had noticed her and had stopped what they were doing to smile and wave. 'They all know how you saved Snowdrop,' Cammie told her, as she waved back. 'Come on! There'll be time to meet them all later. Snowdrop is waiting for you at Queen Mae's house.'

The fairy queen's house was bigger than the others and covered in rambling purple and gold roses. The door was open and when Rosie stepped inside she found herself walking on a carpet of soft petals, which released a beautiful scent as her feet touched them.

In the middle of the room was a large bed made entirely out of red rose petals. Two white petal pillows were propped up at one end and a white sheet – made from lots of white petals sewn together – was draped over the end of the bed.

'Rosie!' a familiar voice called out.

Rosie turned to see Snowdrop skipping towards her, her skin glowing and her blue eyes sparkling as if she had never been ill. She was as tall as Rosie now and her white petal frock seemed to be made from the most enormous petals Rosie had ever seen. She had a patchwork petal shawl draped round her shoulders and her golden hair seemed to have sunlight running through it.

'Snowdrop – you're well again!' Rosie gasped.

'Thanks to you,' Snowdrop beamed, coming over to give Rosie a hug.

It was a strange feeling to have Snowdrop there, the same size as herself. It was just as if Snowdrop were a real child – a friend the same age as herself – rather than a fairy.

'There's so much I want to show you!' Snowdrop laughed, taking Rosie's hand and leading her outside into the fairy village again. 'First the fairy nursery. Come on!'

Snowdrop led her to a long narrow building where little wicker cribs with daisy chains around the edges were lined up along each side. Fairies with white caps and white petal aprons hovered from one crib to the next, checking on their charges.

'Do you want to see a brand new fairy baby?' Snowdrop asked. 'There's one here that's only just been delivered. It's still a bundle of joy really, but it will grow into a baby soon.'

Rosie followed Snowdrop to the first crib and peered inside. She gasped. A cluster of golden sparks was whizzing round and round inside the crib. '*That's* a fairy *baby*?'

'Those sparks will come together to form a fairy soon. Come and see this one. It's the same one you saw that dove bringing to us the other day.'

Rosie followed Snowdrop over to a crib in the centre of the row. Inside was a much bigger cluster of sparks which were stationary and which filled the entire crib. Rosie could see that the shape they formed was that of a little fairy lying on its side, its wings pointing backwards. 'That's amazing!'

'In a few days she'll be ready to leave the nursery,' Snowdrop said. 'There are wee men babies too. Look!' Snowdrop showed her all the babies and introduced her to the fairy nannies.

'The fairy nannies look so kind,' Rosie said as they left the nursery together.

'They are, but it must be very special

having real parents of your own to love you,' Snowdrop replied, sounding wistful.

'I wish Mum and Dad could love *each other* again, not just me,' Rosie sighed. 'Then they'd still be together.'

'Yes, but at least you've *got* a mum and a dad who love you,' Snowdrop persisted. '*Fairies* don't have any parents at all.'

Rosie looked at her friend. She couldn't imagine what it would be like to have *no* parents. 'I suppose I *am* lucky in some ways, aren't I?' she murmured, thinking about it.

'Lucky in some ways and not in others,' Snowdrop said. '*That's* just the same for fairies as it is for humans.' She smiled, grabbing Rosie's hand. 'Come on! Let's go and see the rest of the village now. Then Queen Mae has a present for you.'

So Rosie followed Snowdrop around the village, meeting all the other fairies and their wee men friends, admiring each fairy dwelling place as she passed it. But she couldn't stop thinking about her present and wondering what it could be.

Finally, Snowdrop took her back to Queen Mae's home where the fairy queen was waiting for them. Now that she was the same size as Rosie, she seemed even more stunning. Her shimmery purple dress had miniature thistles embroidered around the neck and a sash of bright yellow sunlight pulling it together at the waist.

'Rosie,' she smiled, coming forward and handing her a single red rose. 'This is to thank you for saving Snowdrop.'

Rosie smelled the rose. It had a beautiful scent. But it wasn't quite what she had been expecting.

'It's a magic rose,' Queen Mae told her. 'You can use it to make a magic wish.'

'A magic wish?'

'That's right.' Queen Mae explained that the wish must be made now because the rose would no longer be magic once it was taken out of the fairy village. 'But you must think carefully before you make your wish, Rosie. It will only work if you wish for something that won't hurt anybody else. Fairy wishes can never be selfish wishes, you see.'

'All right,' Rosie murmured. She thought of the one thing she wanted more than anything else. Then she thought about what Queen Mae had said and whether the other two people involved in her wish would want it to happen too. 'What if I'm not sure whether or not it's the right thing to wish for?' she asked Queen Mae.

'Then think very carefully before you wish for it,' Queen Mae replied.

'But if I don't wish for this to happen . . .' Rosie began, '. . . and Mum and Dad *never*—'

'There are some things that human beings need to sort out for themselves, Rosie,' Queen Mae interrupted her gently. 'Always remember that. And those sorts of things don't usually respond very well to fairy wishes.' She paused. 'What you have to ask yourself is this: is the wish in your head one of those things or not?'

Rosie frowned. She knew the answer to that. And knowing helped her to make her decision.

'I've done it!' she gasped, handing the rose back to Queen Mae. 'Will it come true soon, do you think?'

'Very soon, I expect,' Queen Mae replied, smiling at her kindly. 'And now it is time for you to go home. Cammie and Snowdrop will show you the way. She leaned forward and kissed Rosie on the cheek. 'We will always remember how you helped us, Rosie.'

Rosie felt very tired as she flew between Cammie and Snowdrop back into the village well, down the long tree trunk and out of the forest. Rosie gradually found herself becoming bigger and bigger compared to her two fairy friends, and by the time they reached the tree stump outside the forest, she was back to her normal size.

'You'd better hurry,' Cammie said. 'Old Flora was planning to invite you and your mother round for tea and birthday cake this afternoon.'

'Was she?' Rosie gasped, thinking that that didn't sound a very Flora-like thing to do.

'Save some icing for me, won't you?' Snowdrop said, licking her lips.

'I'll leave some on the window ledge for you tonight,' Rosie promised, suddenly feeling much happier than she had done in a long time. It was beautiful here – much more beautiful than London – and she loved her fairy friends. And if her wish came true then everything was going to be just fine. All she had to do now was go home and see if the fairy magic had worked!

13

Rosie's mum looked happy when Rosie got back to Thistle Cottage, and straight away she told Rosie that she had some good news.

'While you were out earlier, Dad phoned. He says he felt so sad on the way home, not knowing when he was going to get to see you again, that he's booked another flight for four weeks' time. He says he's going to come and see you once a month – either here or you and I will go and meet him in Inverness. What do you think of that?'

'That's brilliant!' Rosie gasped. And it really was brilliant – especially as that hadn't been her fairy wish.

It turned out that Flora had invited Reverend MacKay and his wife to tea as well and they were already there when Rosie and her mum knocked on the door of Flora's cottage.

'Hello, Rosie,' Mrs Mackay said, smiling at her. 'I've been telling my grandaughter, Katie, all about you. She's been moping around all summer because her best friend moved away to the mainland at the end of June. She's the same age as you so I thought you might get along. She wondered if you'd like to go round and play with her tomorrow. I'm going there myself tomorrow morning so I could take you with me if you like.'

Rosie's face lit up. She couldn't believe how many nice things were suddenly happening – with no help at all from her fairy wish. 'Yes, please!' she beamed. 'That's OK, isn't it, Mum?'

Her mother smiled. 'Of course. I've been hoping you'd soon find someone here your own age to play with.'

'Well, I think you and Katie will have plenty in common, Rosie,' Mrs MacKay continued. 'So long as she doesn't drive you mad, telling you about the time she met the queen of the fairies.'

'You mean, Katie's met her too?'

'Aye, so she says . . .' Mrs MacKay exchanged a knowing smile with Rosie's mum. 'She'll tell you all about it herself, I'm sure.'

'Now, who's for a piece of my lovely birthday cake?' Flora said, coming though from the kitchen with a teapot in her hand. She started to cut up the cake, placing a large slice on Rosie's plate and adding an extra piece of icing. 'You can take that away with you if you can't manage it all just now,' she said, giving Rosie a wink.

Rosie winked back – at least Flora knew the fairies were real, even if the other grown-ups didn't.

When she got home, Rosie went straight up to her room and placed the piece of pink icing on her window ledge. Then she went downstairs again to watch some television with her mother.

Later that evening when Rosie opened her bedroom door, Cammie and Snowdrop

were sitting on her bed, munching away at their pink icing supper and giggling together.

Now, at long last, she could test out her fairy wish.

'Mum, come and see!' Rosie cried out.

'What is it?' her mother said, looking over Rosie's shoulder into the room.

'There – on the bed! Can you see them now?' Rosie pointed to her two fairy friends who had stopped munching and were looking at Rosie in surprise.

'I can't see anything except your duvet covered in crumbs of pink icing,' her mother said, a little impatiently. 'I hope you're going to clean that up before you go to bed.'

'But, Mum . . ' Rosie trailed off. There was no point in arguing about it. As soon as her mother had gone, she turned to Cammie and Snowdrop, her face full of disappointment. 'Why didn't my fairy wish work?' she asked them. 'I wished for Mum to be able to see you.'

Snowdrop flew off the bed, back on to the window ledge. She didn't seem too alarmed. 'Don't worry. There's more than one way for a fairy wish to work. You'll see.' She blew Rosie a kiss, smiled her sunniest smile and then she was gone.

When Rosie turned to look, Cammie was gone too. But she could hear him grunting on his top shelf behind the books, so she guessed he was getting himself ready for bed. 'Cammie?' she called out. 'What did Snowdrop mean? *What* other way is there for my fairy wish to work?'

But all she got in reply, a few minutes later, was the sound of snoring.

She had to admit that she felt pretty tired herself and she fell asleep almost as soon as she snuggled down under her duvet.

And when she woke up the next morning, it seemed as if something was different. She couldn't say what exactly, just *something*. She almost expected to look out of the window and find herself back in the middle of London – that's how different she felt.

But when she got up and looked out, she saw her mother sitting in the garden, painting. Everything looked the same. It was a beautiful day and Loch Shee was sparkling in the sunlight. She remembered what had happened the night before and called out Cammie's name but he didn't reply. Either he was still asleep or he had gone to visit his fairy companions in the forest.

Rosie clattered down the stairs, still in her pyjamas, to join her mother out on the lawn.

'Rosie, I had the most amazing dream last night,' her mum called to her excitedly. 'I had to get up straight away and paint it. Come and see!' She was still in her dressing gown and her hair was all bushy where she hadn't bothered brushing it yet. She was holding her paintbrush in one hand as she beckoned Rosie round to her side of the easel.

Rosie took one look at the painting and gasped out loud. There, against a backdrop of dark, starry sky, her mother had painted Snowdrop, Queen Mae and Cammie. She had painted them the same size as they were in real life and their likenesses were so good that anyone would think they had stood and posed for their portraits all night.

Rosie looked from the picture to her mother, unable to conceal her amazement. 'That's *them*! The one in the white dress is Snowdrop . . . the really beautiful one is Queen Mae . . . and the wee man is Cammie.'

Her mum turned her head to smile at Rosie. 'What perfect names for them.'

'I know,' Rosie agreed. 'All the fairies have flower names except Queen Mae—'

'Like you, then,' her mother interrupted her. '*You've* got a flower name too.'

Rosie hadn't thought about that before. She looked again at the picture. It really was perfect.

'Would you like this to hang on your bedroom wall?' her mother asked.

'Oh, yes, please!' Rosie gasped. Then she spotted something. 'Mum, what's that glittery stuff on the end of your brush?'

Her mother looked at the brush. 'What do you mean?'

'It's fairy dust!' Rosie gasped, staring at the tip of the brush in awe.

'Fairy dust?' her mother laughed. 'Oh, Rosie . . . you are funny! That's just some glittery paint I thought I'd try out.' She gave Rosie an indulgent smile. 'You know, I've a feeling that from now on, what with Mrs MacKay's grandaughter to keep you company and Dad visiting more and school starting up in a few weeks, you won't be seeing quite so much of those fairies of yours.'

Rosie was about to protest when she remembered what Queen Mae had said to her when she'd left the fairy village: *We'll never forget you, Rosie . . .*

Had she been saying goodbye? And it was true that Snowdrop had vanished rather suddenly last night and that she hadn't seen Cammie yet this morning.

Still . . . she couldn't imagine her fairy friends leaving her unless she wanted them to.

'You *could* be right, Mum,' she said, running her finger over the end of the paintbrush and getting glittery paint all over her fingertip. 'I don't think so, but . . .' She frowned. For a moment she felt like she didn't really know anything any more. Then she thought of something else and smiled. 'I know, I'll ask Katie what *she* thinks.'

And she ran back upstairs to get dressed, so she'd be ready when Mrs MacKay came to collect her.

Mermaids

Mermaid Magic

Gwyneth Rees

There's a secret world at the bottom of the sea!
Rani came to Tingle Reef when she was a
baby mermaid – she was found fast asleep in a
seashell, and nobody knows where she came
from.

Now strange things keep happening to her –
almost as if by magic. What's going on? Rani's
pet sea horse Roscoe, Octavius the octopus and
a scary sea witch help her find out in these
three stories, *Mermaid Magic, Rani's Sea Spell*
and *The Shell Princess*.

Fairy Treasure

Gwyneth Rees

Connie has never believed in fairies, so she is
amazed when Ruby, a tiny fairy-girl, suddenly
appears in the library of the old house where
Connie is staying.

Ruby says that she is a book fairy – but that she
is in terrible trouble. She has been banished
from fairyland until she finds a ruby ring, which
she has lost.

Can Connie help ruby find the missing ring –
before the doorway to fairyland is closed forever?

Cosmo and the Magic Sneeze
Gwyneth Rees

'A-A-A-TISHOO!' Cosmo burst out, sending a huge shower of magic sneeze into the cauldron.

Cosmo has always wanted to be a witch-cat, just like his father, so when he passes the special test he's really excited. He can't wait to use his magic sneeze to help Sybil the witch mix her spells.

Sybil is very scary, with her green belly button and toenails, and no one trusts her. So when she starts brewing a secret spell recipe – and advertising for kittens – Cosmos and his friend Scarlett begin to worry. Could Sybil be cooking up a truly terrifying spell? And could the extra-special ingredient be KITTENS?

A purrfectly funny and spooky story starring one brave kitten who finds himself in a cauldron-full of trouble.

The Mum Hunt

Gwyneth Rees

Matthew pulled a scornful face. 'How can you miss someone you've never known?'

Esmie does miss her mum, even though she was only a tiny baby when she died. She has a photo by her bed – and sometimes, when she needs advice or just fancies a chat, she asks her mum for help. Sometimes she even hears her reply.

But Esmie thinks her dad is lonely. And her big brother Matthew would definitely benefit from a female influence. So Esmie decides to take action – she's going to find her dad a girlfriend. Beautiful, clever, charming, kind to children and animals . . . How hard can it be to find the perfect partner for your dad?